D1471696

I dedicate this book to my nephew, Oliver.
I hope one day you read this and enjoy it as much as I did
writing it.

Maximilian Fritz: The Teenage Superhero

T. J. Crossley

CONTENTS

ACKNOWLEDGMENTS

There are a lot of people I'm thankful for who helped and inspired me to finish this little story. But the people I'd like to mention here are my parents... Their steadfast love, and boundless energy have kept me going...

1

Maximilian Fritz squinted as he looked at the algebra homework. The equations on the page looked more blurry than usual. He tried to focus. *Was that a 6 or an 8...?* he wondered as he leaned further into the page, *and was that a 2 or a 7?*

Max slunk down onto the floor. In the shaded side alley of the busy city of Chicago, he was engulfed in the sound of shouts and horns echoing from the nearby busy street. Max turned the page of his textbook.

The familiar voice of Luigi from the local pizzeria next door rang out. 'Hey Stella,' he said. 'Have you got the flour?'

Pulling out a pen from his bag he began to scribble down some notes for the Math questions that were due for tomorrow. A stray cat slipped by, rubbing his back against Max's arm. *Was that a 9 or an 8?* he wondered, squinting back at his textbook. *Maybe his mother was right?* he thought. *Maybe he did need glasses after all.* The truth is Max wasn't that keen on the idea of getting them. *They might call me four eyes,* he thought, thinking about his classmates from school. And the way his sister put her contacts on every morning with the eye drops and the thin lens, that didn't much appeal to Max either.

The smell of pizza wafted through the side alley as Max continued to try to read. He had been going to the pizzeria for over two years now, to grab a slice after school and to say hi to Luigi and his wife.

'I like you kid,' Luigi would say as he would hand Max the free slice of pizza over a paper napkin. It was a time of catching up and Luigi's jokes.

Max looked at his watch, just five minutes to go before his Taekwondo lesson. He shuddered and shut his textbook, even his watch was looking blurry.

4

Now inside the dojo, Max finished his session with an impressive double kick in the air. Beads of sweat trickled down his forehead.

'Wow Max,' said Jason, his trainer. 'You're getting better.'

Max smiled. He had been working on the kicks at home in the backyard. It seemed like his practice was paying off. Max was tall for a fifteen-year-old which made his kicks even more striking, thought Jason, his trainer. It was the end of the session, the students stopping what they were doing, some more out of breath than others.

'You guys have done really well today,' said Jason as he looked at the long line of teens in their Taekwondo outfits with belts and bare feet.

Max slung his backpack over his back as he ran out of the backdoor of the dojo. Before he even had time to think he felt himself bump shoulders with someone who was trying to get in.

'What's up Bozo?' said the person. Max turned around. It was Jake Harris from school.

'Hi Jake,' said Max timidly, shifting past Jake, looking to get away.

'So this is where your Taekwondo lessons are, eh?' said Jake peering into the dojo. 'Hey Max—' called Jake.

Max was midway down the alley by now. Two of Jake's friends were standing with him. Reluctantly Max turned around.

'So Max…' said Jake slowly. 'Can you show me some then?' he said, nudging both of his friends as they started to laugh quietly.

Max stood silent.

'Well?' said Jake.

'You mean the Taekwondo?' said Max.

Jake nodded. There was a pause… then slowly Max readied himself… before striking out with a double kick. Immediately he wished he had performed the kick better; he WAS wearing jeans and t-shirt and had his backpack on.

Slowly, Jake started to laugh again, his two friends joining in.

'Girl—' came the voice of Jake, the three continuing in hysterics.

'Listen guys,' said Max finally, 'I gotta go, ok?'

'Max,' called Jake again as Max ran down the alley. Reluctantly Max turned around once more. 'Stick to your science books—' said Jake in a fit of hysterics, the two others laughing with him.

'He's probably just jealous of you,' said Max's mum, Jenny, pouring her son a cup of chocolate milk.

6

Max sighed. 'Well it wasn't cool,' said Max. 'They just stood there laughing at me. I looked like an idiot.'

Jenny handed Max the cup. 'Sometimes… sometimes you gotta ignore those types of people. You know, not let them get to you,' she said.

Max nodded, but he found it difficult to agree. *Why can't everyone just be nice?* he wondered.

'Why don't you get yourself ready for bed,' Jenny said finally, patting Max on the back as he finished gulping down his favourite evening drink.

'Alright mum,' said Max. Max tiptoed upstairs so as not to disturb his father who was working in the office. His father Wayne, worked tirelessly at the banks in central Chicago and Jenny would always make sure her son was quiet when going upstairs.

Max pulled the bedcovers over himself. He reached for a torch and a book on his side table. Flicking on the light he looked at the front cover. It was a large book he had recently borrowed from the library. *Earth's Wild Cats* read the cover, as slowly Max turned the first page.

Then it started to happen again. The words he was reading started to blur. Max sighed. He was going to have to do something about his eyesight.

7

'Max, it's time to wake up,' came the voice of Jenny, slowly Max opening his eyes. He saw his mother standing there with her usual big grin on her face. 'It's a new day Max. Up and at 'em.'

'What time is it?' said Max, slowly getting out of bed.

'Time for school don't you think?'

Just as his mum was about to leave the room.

'Hey Mum—' said Max. Max looked at the book on the side table, then back to his mum. 'I think, I think I need glasses… I guess… I guess I'm struggling to read.'

'Oh that's ok Honey,' said Jenny, with a comforting tone, 'I thought that might be the case. It's alright, I'll book an opticians appointment for you sometime today.'

******

Max made his way from the bus to the entrance of the school.

'Hi Max,' said Mr. Pierce, one of Max's favourite teachers, a Geography teacher, who was waiting outside on monitoring duty, the kids making their way through the entrance to Chicago High. The sun was shining as Max entered the main square of the school and over to his registration classroom.

Apart from the fact that Max struggled to read his textbooks, things went well for him that day. Max scored a nine out of ten for a recent science test and was to learn he was to do a presentation for his 'Topic' class on the subject of anything he wanted.

'You have an umpteen selection of interesting things to choose from,' said the teacher as he scanned the classroom. 'You can choose anything you want.'

'Hi Max,' came a voice, Max sitting there eating his Italian lunch at the diner. It was Max's good friend Chuck. Chuck side-stepped around the table sitting opposite to Max. 'I see you got the lasagne,' said Chuck. 'Thought I'd help myself to some of the bolognese. Did you know Italians have over three hundred and fifty pasta types?'

Max shook his head.

'Yeah,' said Chuck. 'It's true, Lucy from the diner told me.'

'You know what you're going to do for the topic presentation yet?' asked Max.

'No, not yet,' said Chuck. 'But I was thinking of maybe doing someone like Nelson Mandela.'

Max nodded. 'That's a good idea,' he said.

Chuck pulled out his gameboy. The little handheld game blared out tinny, bouncy music.

9

'Hey Chuck,' said Max.

'Uhuh?'

'You wanna come to the mall with me this weekend? I'm going to the opticians to get my eyes checked. My mum said it would be for just half an hour and after that we could check out the mall. I'm thinking we could go to the arcade. You wanna come?'

'Sure,' said Chuck.

******

'Now boys,' said Jenny as they got out of the car. We'll be just thirty minutes, which gives us plenty of time afterwards to explore the mall and get some ice-cream.' It was an unusually hot day and Jenny was wearing her sunglasses. She nudged Max. 'Is that ok?'

'Of course,' said Max.

The downtown mall was one of Max's favourite places to be. There were lifts that ascended to the fifth floor, water fountains and the echo of children, candy machines, candy floss and pretzels, but the best thing about the mall Max thought, were the sports shops. Max was a big fan of basketball sneakers. Max loved the different colours and the feel of the shoes. His favourite make were the 'Jordans' because of the unique logo and their finished shine. Max enjoyed playing basketball at school and because of his height his PE teacher always encouraged him to play as much as he could, alongside Taekwondo.

The opticians went by in a flash and soon enough Max found himself free to explore the mall with Chuck, giving them just enough time to play in the arcade before he was to meet his mum at the entrance. Max knew exactly where he wanted to go first.

It was like being in a candy store to Max. All the different sports equipment as well as the basketball sneakers that even some of the NBA stars wore. Max looked at the price of a pair of shoes that had caught his eye. A pair of white Jordans he knew were some of the best out there. $200 dollars. He would have to wait a year or two before he could buy them. But he knew he'd get them eventually. Max looked around all the other departments with Chuck. The golf section, the tennis section, but before he left there was still one area that awaited him.

Max ran his fingers down the white cloth as he set his eyes on the 'dobok' along with belt. He looked at the different sizes ranging for the youngest of persons to the biggest. There on the wall by the 'doboks' was a large picture of a famous female fighter who recently competed at the last Olympic Games representing the USA.

Max looked at his watch, they had just twenty minutes to go before they were to meet his mum by the entrance. Leaving the shop they walked swiftly towards the arcade.

Pow, Pow, Pow— went the laser guns as Max and Chuck flicked their aim this way and that. The screen flashed as the zombies trudged their way towards where the two boys were standing. It was 'Zombies of the Apocalypse,' and it was the boys' favourite game at the arcade.

2

Before long it was time for them to head back. Just as they had nearly reached the entrance to the mall, suddenly to his right Max heard a scream from a store making him jump! Then he saw something that he had never seen before. There in the jewellery store Max saw what appeared to be a man holding a woman behind the counter at gunpoint! He was wearing a grey balaclava and had come out of nowhere. Other people in the shop huddled behind the jewellery counters as the man began to point the gun in all directions. 'Don't move!' he shouted.

Max's first instinct was to put his arm in-front of Chuck to protect him.

'Follow me,' whispered Max after a few moments. Chuck and Max huddled into a shop opposite, hiding behind some shoe shelves, other people frozen around the store, some people running away, others not daring to move. There were shouts and whimperings from onlookers as some pointed to the thief in the store. Quickly the lady behind the counter offered up the diamonds, the man with the gun stuffing them into his bag. In no more than a few seconds the thief ran out of the shop and out of the mall. Seconds later the alarms went off all around.

'Honey, you boys got me so worried!' cried Jenny, seeing floods of people coming out of the mall, eventually noticing Max and Chuck. Security officers and a few policemen were already on the scene trying to answer any questions that were being thrown around. 'What is happening?' she exclaimed as Max and Chuck ran over to her.

'Mum!' exclaimed Max, the pair meeting with a hug, Chuck standing by.

'Are you boys alright?'

'Mum, I saw the whole thing!' said Max. 'I saw the thief, and he was holding a gun!'

'Oh my!' exclaimed the mother. 'Are you guys ok?'

'We're fine,' said Max.

'We need to go home right now,' she said finally, giving them hugs then huddling them into the car.

'And you're telling me the man had a gun!' cried Wayne looking at Jenny and then to his son in the kitchen that night. Max nodded, taking a sip of some more of his chocolate milk.

'That's terrible,' Wayne said, walking over to the fridge to get himself some orange juice. 'Well,' he said eventually, 'some people go out of their way to get what they want, even if it means going against the law. It's just a shame that it had to happen here in Chicago.' He shook his head. 'And in broad daylight too.'

'Alright son,' said the dad finally. 'You better go upstairs and do your homework. It's been a long day for us all.'

Just then there was a knock at the door. Max's mum went to see who it was. Max saw two men in police uniforms there at the front door, Jenny nodding as they continued to talk to her.

Eventually Wayne made his way over. The four continued talking quietly.

That night Max did his homework, but he couldn't stop thinking about what went on in the mall and how it made him feel.

14

The next morning things were as normal. Max had gotten himself up and made his way downstairs.

'Now Max, tell me what you're going to do after school today,' Jenny said, Max with a mouth full of his favourite cheerios.

'Don't worry mum,' said Max. 'I haven't forgotten.'

'Good, remember the police station is on 34th Street. It's just a two-minute walk from the dojo. You'll remember that Honey won't you?'

'Thanks Mum,' said Max.

'Oh Honey… I'm so proud of you,' said Jenny. 'I'm so glad you were safe yesterday. Things could have been worse you know.'

'I know,' said Max.

'Have a good day at school,' she said, Max opening the front door to catch the bus.

Shutting the door behind Max could see Chuck running down the road as the pair made their way over to the bus stop.

'You ready to talk to the police after school today?' said Chuck, a little out of breath, the pair climbing aboard the bus. 'They came around my house too, they caught us on the cameras you know. They said we had one of the best views of the crime scene yesterday at the mall.'

15

'I know,' said Max. The thought of it all gave Max the shivers.

The time at the police station was a little more sombre than Max had anticipated. Very early on Max was ushered into a private room, passing busy policemen and officials taking phone calls, working at their desks through the windows. Inside the room were three police officers sitting, looking very serious, before one of them spoke.

Max sat quietly.

'So Max, can you tell us what you saw yesterday at the mall?'

The questions continued. 'Did you see anyone suspicious looking before you heard the scream?'

At one point Max didn't know what to think, but tried his best to answer the questions as well as he could. Twenty minutes went by, then the interview ended.

'Well that was something,' said Chuck, the pair finally meeting together again at the reception of the police station. 'What did they ask you?' said Chuck as they started to walk towards the dojo.

'What we saw at the mall,' said Max. 'I told them I saw a guy with a grey balaclava over his head. He was wearing jeans and a black long-sleeve t-shirt, pointing a gun at the shop assistant. What did you say?'

'Pretty much the same thing,' said Chuck.

Max gave everything he got towards the final punches and kicks of his Taekwondo class that evening.

'Good Max,' said the teacher, patting him on the back. 'Those were some great kicks at the end there Max. You always try so hard, I like that about you Max. You're so committed.'

That afternoon after class Max didn't much feel like talking to his friends from the lesson. He was tired from the exercise and the truth is he had tried as hard as he could at class to keep his mind off what had happened at the mall and at the police station. Chuck had even offered to stay and watch the lesson for an hour, while Max practised, to which Max had agreed was fine. But even after the class Max didn't feel like talking to Chuck much either. For some reason Max felt like keeping himself to himself. Max's plan was to quickly grab a bite from Luigi's pizza, then go home.

Just as Max and Chuck and some of the other students were leaving the dojo, much to Max's disappointment, Jake appeared again down the alley with two of his friends. 'Hey Bozo,' shouted Jake, towards Max.

Jake and his two friends made their way towards where Chuck and Max were standing. 'Hey Max,' said Jake, 'I thought I told you to stick to science books.'

'Sorry Jake, but I don't have time for this,' said Max, side-stepping around the three who were blocking his way.

'Hey, get back here kid!' said Jake reaching out and grabbing Max's arm. Max instantly felt a rush of anger, throwing back Jake's arm the way it came. Then with a flash of anger Jake swung out with his fist narrowly missing a punch directed towards Max's face. Max ducked and instinctually readied himself into a typical Taekwondo pose. There were a few moments of stillness, the sun shining in the late afternoon.

'Run,' shouted Max as Chuck quickly skidded past the three boys, leaving them in their tracks. Jake and his two friends watched as the two boys scrambled away.

That evening Max didn't want to talk to anyone. Quietly he opened the door to his house, his parents in the living room, watching the news. Max crept behind the sofa and towards the kitchen, his parents barely noticing him. The newsreader's voice rang out, 'News just in. There has been an account of a brutal shooting in downtown Chicago this evening. Our reporter James McMillan is there on the scene.'

18

Just then Wayne sensed Max standing behind him. He turned around. '—Max, why don't you get yourself some pizza, there's still some left on the counter.'

Max nodded, taking a piece before making his way up the stairs to his room.

That night Max didn't feel good inside. The robbery at the mall had affected him. Jake Harris had affected him. Even the news had affected him. He slunk back in his bed before he was to fall asleep. To be honest Max didn't feel great at all. And so he reached for his book from the library and grabbed his torch and started to turn the pages. It was the book about wild cats. He read about the lynxes cat that could be found in North America, Europe and Asia. He read about the African lions and the tigers that originated from the jungles of India. It wasn't until Max was starting to feel very tired that he stopped what he was doing and yawned momentarily. Before him was the page of the Snow Leopard.

There was something about this cat that fascinated Max… and yet Max could feel himself falling asleep. Max continued to read what he could, but the yawns kept coming. 'With only an estimate of 4000 - 5,600 left in the wild,' he read, 'the snow leopard is an endangered species. They weigh in at around 60 - 120 lbs.' Max yawned again. 'The snow

19

leopard is responsible for being the animal that can jump further than any other in the world. With a vertical jump of over six metres and horizontal of fifteen metres, it's fair to say the Snow Leopard has an innate 'jumping ability.' The longest jump observed by a snow leopard was more than forty-nine feet. Even longer than the average length of a school bus.'

Max couldn't read anymore, he was just too tired, and so finally he drifted to sleep.

That night the thunder and rain came, contrasting from the heat of the day. Like the gods of the sky had aligned and had decided to reign their fury over the town, the lightning tore through the night-sky; Max lying fast-asleep in bed.

3

The only source of light within the vicinity of the club was an electric one, hanging just above the doorway. There, underneath the railway arches in Chicago was located a little place where people would meet to play pool, use the slot machines and maybe play some poker. It wasn't exactly the nicest place in town.

There, a man is kicked out of the entrance of the small club. Another man makes his way out to where the first has fallen onto the ground, groaning and turning on the roadside.

'Like I said, if you can't pay, don't play,' says the second man towering above the man on the ground.

The second man looks about ready to kick the man laying there, when suddenly the first man calls out. 'Wait—' he says, 'I'll give you the money by Thursday.'

'No can do,' says the second man, and then in a fit of rage begins to kick the man on the ground, the man calling out in pain.

There is a pause as the second man stops. He towers over the man, groaning. The eerie light over the doorway casts a shadow on the road where the two men are. Then strangely, the man on the ground begins to laugh, first quietly and then into loud hysterics, rolling over. His laughter gets louder, then even louder, confusing the man standing above him.

'The city doesn't deserve you,' says the second man at long last. The second man turns away and re-enters the club, slamming the door behind him.

With the last ounce of energy the first man has, he shouts, laying, rolling on the ground, 'No, you're right... Chicago doesn't deserve me!'

21

******

The morning light of Chicago shines through the crack in the curtains of the third house on Brompton Road, the home of Maximilian Fritz. Max is woken by the bright sunlight covering his eyes. He sits up and feels the book he was reading slip onto the floor. For some reason Max feels better than normal as he stands up and stretches. He makes his way over to the window where the front lawn is, still wet from the thunder and rain last night. Quietly Max hears a knock at the door.

'I'm already up,' says Max, the door gently opening, Jenny standing there, smiling.

Quietly Max readies his things as he gets himself prepared for his day of school.

His mum is waiting in the kitchen. She begins to serve him some pancakes and waffles she had prepared earlier. 'Did you hear the thunder last night?' she said. 'It got pretty loud didn't it?'

Max nodded.

'What lessons have you got today?' asked the mum.

'Oh nothing much. Just Maths and Topic for the first two. Nothing special,' said Max. 'Mum?' said Max all of a sudden, 'These pancakes taste great.'

22

'Well thanks Dear,' said Jenny. 'Don't think I changed the recipe around or anything. Just the same as usual. But glad you think so,' she said. 'Now don't be late for the bus.'

Max got up from the stool and grabbed his bag and headed towards the front door. Just as he opened the door he saw the bus driving down the road.

'Oh Max,' said Jenny quickly. 'I've got something for you.' She handed him a glasses case.

Slowly Max opened the case and put the pair of glasses on. Now he could see perfectly, including reading the time from his watch. 'Thanks mum,' he said.

Max ran over to where the bus stop was, the fresh-air around him, feeling inspired more than usual. Chuck was already there at the bus stop. Together the two slipped onto the bus. Gradually the wheels started to turn as Max and Chuck made their way down the aisle. Max recognized all the faces that normally rode the bus that morning, all apart from a girl with dark, brown hair who sat quietly towards the back on the right side. She looked pretty, thought Max and if anything possessed a slightly petite figure. There was a space next to her as well as a seat opposite. Max took the seat next to the girl, Chuck sitting on the other side. Max could smell the girl's perfume.

'Hey Klara,' said one of the girls from behind their row. 'Got any gum?'

'I see you've made some friends already,' said Max, looking over to the new girl kindly.

'I guess,' she smiled.

'Sure,' she said. Reaching for her backpack, she pulled out some gum from the front pocket and handed it to the girl behind.

'Now class, I want you to remember the topic presentation that's due next week,' said Mr. Giles as he walked down through the single desks of the classroom. 'I want you to remember the requirements that must be met when doing the presentation.' Max sat there listening to what the teacher had to say. He felt a buzz in his body too, an urge to run a mile. He felt excited, happy. Something about him felt different that morning. 'Now class,' said the teacher. 'Remember it's due Thursday next week.' Then the bell rang and the students got up to get ready for lunch.

'I could eat twelve dinners right now,' said Max to Chuck making their way towards the diner. The two lined up as they got nearer to the food. Max felt a rumble in his stomach, piling on a quarter chicken, gravy and some potato onto his plate. Chuck following took a can of his favourite soda, opening it, then grabbed some food for himself.

The two made their way over to where their usual spot was. Unfortunately, thanks to bad timing Jake could be seen with his two friends walking down the main diner aisle which divided the rows of tables either side. Jake seizing his opportunity nudged Chuck as they brushed past. Chuck lost his balance, letting go of his tray of food which had the can of soda on it. Chuck nearly fell to the ground as the food and the tray flew from his hands, the can of soda flying into the air spilling onto nearby students. Everyone stopped what they were doing. Max quickly grabbed Jake. 'Jake, what was that for?' exclaimed Max, Jake starting to laugh.

'I'm sorry Max, it was an accident. What do you want me to say?'

Then Max felt a sudden feeling of frustration and anger towards Jake more than he had ever felt before. Like a lightning bolt had struck him and filled him with energy, he struck out at Jake, performing a typical Taekwondo punch he learnt from class. What happened next sent shivers down people's spines. Max punched Jake in the chest, sending him flying down the aisle a good twelve feet or so into the double doors — crashing onto the floor where he lay in complete shock. The whole room went quiet. Max looked at himself and then to everyone watching. Then he ran away.

Max ran out the entrance of the school and down the road, running like a bloodhound. *Why did Jake have to do that to Chuck? And how had Jake managed to have flown that far along the aisle of the diner when he hit him? Did he have super strength?*

Soon enough Max stopped running, stopping outside a gas station.

'Hey kid,' came the voice of someone. Max turned around.

'Shouldn't you be at school kid?' came the voice of a policeman making his way over to where Max was.

'What were you thinking Max?' said the principal sitting there at his desk, looking at the notes that were given to him. He looked up at Max, who sat opposite.

'Sir, I really don't know what came over me. I felt like what Jake did to Chuck, with his tray of food and everything, was on purpose. But I mean, I guess I didn't mean to hit Jake so hard. I mean…'

'Max,' said the principal. 'It says here that you punched him, some of the students saying Jake flew back a good twelve feet or so after impact. Whether I believe that or not, I'm not sure I do. But it sounds like it was a hard punch you gave Jake, Max?' There was a pause in the conversation.

26

'You do Taekwondo don't you?' said the principal looking at the boy.

Max nodded. Max's face looked solemn. 'Taekwondo is an Olympic sport sir…' said Max, slowly.

'Listen,' said the principal after a good few moments of silence. 'Max, you're so normally well-behaved. You always have had good school reports. But I'm afraid something must be done about this. I'm sorry Max,' said the principal. 'I'm afraid it's detention for a week.'

That afternoon Max went to his room without talking to his parents. The school had already phoned his mum and told her what had happened at the diner. Max's mum stood outside his bedroom door. 'You didn't have to punch him Max. You know you can tell others in charge if someone is harassing you. I know it's not cool to do something like that nowadays, but really it's the only way. Oh Max you've always been such a good boy,' she said. Max kept quiet, keeping his bedroom door locked.

The following morning Max woke up with a small headache. He couldn't stop thinking about what happened yesterday, at the diner, how he had punched Jake and sent him flying back into the double doors. The very thought of it gave Max the shivers. *How did he manage to do such a thing? He knew he was good at Taekwondo, yet he wasn't that strong enough to send Jake flying back twelve feet or so by just a single punch?*

Max made his way down the stairs as he heard his mother in the kitchen preparing breakfast. The eggs sizzled on the pan, toast popping up from the toaster. 'Mum, do you mind if I go outside?' said Max.

'Sure Honey,' she said.

'Oh Max, um, don't forget today is the first day of your… um…'

'Detention? Don't worry mum,' said Max, 'I won't forget.'

Max had a thirty-minute wait in the back garden before the bus was to come. Max, wanting to see if he could mimic the punch he had done on Jake yesterday, stood in the middle of the garden and readied himself, before releasing his fist. Nothing happened that was any different to how he'd normally punch. Max tried again, and then again, but Max did not feel anything particularly different to how he'd normally do it. He punched out again, and then again, and all of it felt normal.

'Max, you're gonna miss the bus,' called Jenny from the backdoor.

'Max, I wanted to tell you something,' said Chuck as they sat there at the diner table at lunch. 'Thank you,' he said, slowly putting a spoon full of trifle dessert into his mouth. 'Thank you for looking out for me. You know, yesterday, with Jake and all.'

'It's ok,' said Max.

'I know it got you detention for a week… but thanks anyway,' Chuck said sincerely.

After his detention Max took the bus into Chicago city centre for his afternoon Taekwondo lesson. He was already fifteen minutes late. Maybe he could catch the last thirty minutes of the lesson, if only the driver was quicker.

Stepping off the bus he made his way down the side alley towards the dojo. Making his way down the alley, Max heard a familiar voice.

'Hey Max—'

Max turned around. There was Jake again with two of his friends, except there was a large smile on Jake's face that looked particularly menacing. Quickly the three boys made their way around Max, cornering him. Max froze.

'What you did yesterday was not cool Max,' said Jake looking him directly in the eye. In one quick move Jake lashed out at Max swinging a punch directly for his face.

Max ducked just in time.

29

'Get him!' cried Jake.

At first Max didn't know what to do. Then suddenly, Max did something he never thought he would do. He jumped. He jumped upwards at least a good twenty feet or so, catching himself on the edge of the top of the dojo that made the left side of the alley. For a few moments he stayed up there, clinging to the top, looking down as the three boys stared in utter amazement. Max stayed up there for a few more moments then let go and fell again landing perfectly onto the ground. The boys said nothing, standing in absolute amazement.

'Freak!?' said Jake suddenly as he beckoned to the two of his friends. Together the three backed off, skidding and running down the alley as fast as they could.

Max stood there still. He watched as the boys ran away, and then looked at his arms and his hands and his feet. *What just happened? Was he dreaming?* He pinched himself to see if he was asleep. Nothing happened.

Then there was a sudden and slow sense of excitement that came upon him that made him begin to wonder. *What if I could do that again?* And so he jumped. But it wasn't very high. He jumped again. The same thing happened. This time he closed his eyes and readied himself to jump as high as he could possibly go.

WHOOSH— went Max as he flew up to the top of the building clutching the topside of the dojo as before. Then letting go he landed perfectly on the ground.

Max ran and ran to Chicago's biggest park. He felt a release in himself running as fast as he could, feeling a buzz right from the top of his head to the soles of his feet. He ran, darting through people on the sidewalks of the city centre, until finally he reached Lincoln Park.

Making his way to a more secluded area where there were trees, he jumped, clutching onto the top branches, jumping down from them. It wasn't only his ability to jump high either. He quickly discovered he could jump long too. He started to jump as far as he could, maybe twenty metres or so in the distance within the seclusion of the trees. It wasn't until about twenty minutes later that Max decided to do the ultimate thing. He ran out into the massive open space of the park and running as fast as he could propelled himself into the air where he soared upwards a good twenty to thirty feet or so, approximately seventy-five yards in length, gliding along as far as he could, like a football. Landing on the ground again, he quickly turned around to see if anybody was watching him from the paths. But at the same time he didn't care. He turned around and ran as fast as he could and jumped back the way he came. There was such a buzz and excitement in Max that he couldn't help but shout for joy as he flew through the air.

That night Max lay in bed, feeling a great sense of excitement and even disbelief about what had happened the past few days. His punch towards Jake and then the jumping outside the dojo, and then in the park! *What did this all mean?* he wondered. One thing he did know was that he would keep it quiet just for now. The last thing he wanted was some sort of newfound fame, or even worse, being detained. Max had the idea that if he was to tell someone so soon, something bad might happen. Still, Max felt better than ever.

******

Max trudged along the halls of his school, people pushing and shoving as they went this way and that, the majority of them getting their things to go home. Still, Max felt the urge to be outside. It had nearly been twenty-four hours since Max had realised his newfound jumping ability, and to be honest Max was still unsure if it was possible for him to repeat what had happened yesterday, or if he was still just dreaming. Or perhaps none of it had really happened at all, maybe he was sick and imagining things. Max still had so many questions, yet unfortunately now was not the time for it was Max's second day of detention. And so he waited for people to pass through the hallways, stepping into the detention room.

There were other people already there, some of them likely to be for just the one afternoon, others who might be on a more regular basis. Max walked inside and took a seat. The teacher at the front of the room with her laptop and a cup of coffee sipped loudly on her drink before saying. 'Guys I'm just gonna be ten minutes. Please no misbehaving while I'm gone.' At first the class was silent, no one particularly sure if any of them should speak. Max looked to his right and saw what appeared to be the 'typical detention boy' sitting at the back beginning to throw bits of screwed up paper at a girl sitting in front of him.

'Would you cut it out?' she said finally, turning around.

'Oooh, alright then,' said the boy.

Just at that moment a girl entered the room, dressed in all black. She had a short black skirt with purple hair in two pigtails and a cartoon skull and crossbones on her t-shirt.

Max recognized her from his year but his class was so big, he didn't really know her name.

'So how many days' detention have you guys got?' she said as she looked around, pulling out a pocket mirror from

33

her bag, smacking her lips together. Slowly she turned to each one in the classroom.

Most of the students said just one, occasionally two. Then came Max.

'Five,' said Max.

'Five!?' she said, trying to conceal her surprise. 'And what did you do to get five?' she chuckled, finally.

'I was the guy that punched Jake,' said Max.

The girl started to blush. 'Oh wow,' she said. 'So it was you!?'

Next to answer was the boy at the back of the class who looked like he had been in the room many times before. 'Dare I ask?' she whispered.

That afternoon Max took the bus to the centre of Chicago where he went back to Lincoln Park. He stayed out all evening jumping from tree to tree, jumping out into the wide open of the fields when he was certain no one was looking. His wish had come true, his ability to jump had stayed, and yet he didn't want to tell anyone, not yet.

Back at home Max turned the page of his encyclopaedia, rummaging through some of the books on his shelves. *What did he want to do for his topic presentation?* he wondered, realising that it was due in just a few days' time. Quietly he sifted through his books looking at all the autobiographies he had, one about Muhammad Ali, another on Florence Nightingale 'The Founder of Modern Nursing' and then another about Christopher Columbus who discovered the Americas in 1492. Half of the books he hadn't even read yet. Sifting through his magazines, books and browsing the internet there was nothing that particularly sparked his imagination. It wasn't until he found himself turning through the pages of one of his sports magazines that he got the idea. There on the page was a signed red jersey of the Chicago Bulls, a 90's vintage piece. *Of course,* he thought to himself, *I'll do Michael Jordan.* A smile grew on his face as he thought about what he and Michael Jordan had in common, the ability to jump.

The wind soared through Max's face the following afternoon as he ran and jumped and flew through Lincoln Park. Soon enough Max began to run further out of the city, where there was more space, always keeping a lookout to see that nobody was watching him. He would jump as far as he could through open car parks and empty roads, propelling himself into the air. Then Max, tempted to go back to the inner city of Chicago and try to jump on top of buildings that were around, jumped onto the roofs of grocery stores, cinemas, running over their flat roofs,

35

inventing his own kind of 'parcours.' He even jumped onto the police station but quickly realising what type of building it was jumped off again. Max estimated that he could jump up to a height of fifty feet or so into the air. It was a good evening all in all.

4

The man lay there on the ground silent, whining and moaning in pain. He rolled from one side to the other, his hands holding his stomach, looking like he was about to be sick. The electric light outside the club buzzed and spat. Gradually, conjuring the strength, he groaned, placing an arm onto the road, the faint sound of music blaring from the club. Standing to his feet he hobbled and wretched in pain. The sound of the chitter chattering of a train passed by, lifting the silence, as it went directly to the centre of Chicago. He hobbled along the streets in the direction of the train, the black of the night sky blanketing the horizon with just the lights of people's homes and offices still intact.

******

The day was a Thursday and Max had just made it to school on time before the front gates at the entrance were locked. Chuck was waiting behind the school gates as they made their way to their registration class. 'Didn't you hear?' said Chuck, 'We're going on a trip to the West Coast. At the end of the term. To California! In two weeks! Mr. Pierce said we're gonna be studying the salt levels in Death Valley. California here we come,' exclaimed Chuck, the two making their way inside.

Low and behold Chuck was right. At the end of Mr. Pierce's Geography lesson, just before everyone was to pack up their things, Mr. Pierce hushed the class. 'So class,' he said, 'I can confirm the rumours are true. We will be going to California to visit Death Valley. We will be looking at the salt levels of the desert floor. Now, Death Valley is largely a desert plain and notoriously hot, so I don't want any of you getting dehydrated when we're out there. Your safety is our utmost importance, so we'll be bringing lots of water and sun cream everywhere we go. Mr. Durham and Miss. Stephens will be joining us. And it's not only Death Valley we'll be visiting, there'll be time for you to see some of California's great coasts too, including California's St. Monica Pier. Now who thinks this sounds like fun?'

Before Mr. Pierce had any time to finish speaking, the classroom started talking again, a whir of excitement growing in the air as some students started to cheer. 'California!' exclaimed some, as gradually everyone began to file out of the classroom.

'Start thinking about packing your bags!' exclaimed Mr. Pierce as the students clambered through the door. It's in just two weeks!'

Max had never been to California before but knew well about the basketball teams that were there as well as the amusement parks and the great coastlines. 'Mum,' exclaimed Max entering the kitchen that afternoon, 'Did you know? We'll be going to California for a school trip, in exactly two weeks. Isn't that awesome?' he cried.

'Oh Honey, sounds wonderful,' said Jenny. 'I'll have to help you pack.'

The following day was a Thursday which meant it was time for Max to do his presentation on Michael Jordan. He had prepared for it late into the evening the previous night. Things went well for him, the teacher giving him an eight out of ten. 'You could do with lifting your voice a little louder,' she said, delivering her verdict for each and every student. Chuck also got an eight for his presentation which he was pleased with. The day went by quickly, and before Max had even time to realise his detention was nearing a close, the bell rang for four o'clock which meant he was free to go home. The sunset was in the sky as Max took the bus into the city streets of Chicago, running down the side alleys, he jumped off the side of the walls propelling himself twenty feet or so into the air landing perfectly back onto his feet. He enjoyed jumping onto the roofs of one and two storey buildings, one of his favourite locations being a local Burger King in the city centre where he would hide behind the sign on the top of roof, the city skyline before him, and watch as the sunset would go down.

5

The man stopped what he was doing, putting the tomato soup can back, huddling close to the shelves listening to what he could hear from the other side of the convenience store. If the man was right, he should be entering about now.

A few moments later a man walked through the door, the doorbell ringing, making his way over to the counter. The first man stopped and waited, pretending to rummage through the breads peering around to where the counter was; hiding his face from the security cameras placed in the top two corners of the convenience store. The man working behind the counter had his back facing the customer, stretching up to the glass shelves where the nicotine and cigarettes were placed. 'Can I help you?' he said at last, turning around. To his shock what he saw next made him jump back in fear. Immediately he put his hands in the air.

The customer was wearing a balaclava with a firearm pointed directly at him. 'Open your register,' said the man with the balaclava. 'Give me all your cash.'

It was at that moment that the man hiding behind the aisle quietly stepped out towards the counter where the shop assistant was held hostage holding out a firearm of his own. 'CPD, you're under arrest,' came the voice of the man at the back. He reached for his pocket and dropped his CPD ID for the guy behind the counter to see.

The shop assistant behind the counter nodded in approval, watching as the policeman dragged away the criminal caught in the middle.

'Let go of me!' cried the man as they stumbled down the road towards the policeman's car.

'Listen, why don't you shut up for two seconds,' whispered the cop into the man's ear. 'I'm here to help you.'

'Help me?' cried the second man, 'it doesn't much look like you're doing that?'

******

'Alright alright—' said Mr. Pierce as he counted the students that were stepping onto the coach. 'We gotta go soon if we're gonna catch this flight.'

'Why did I not bring a bag with wheels?' exclaimed Chuck as he trudged towards the coach, Max at his side with his own suitcase on wheels.

'It's alright,' said Mr. Pierce, helping Chuck throw his bag into the luggage section. 'We'll get something at the airport for you.'

'Wait!' cried a voice from behind.

'Don't forget about me—' came the voice. It was Klara wheeling her suitcase towards the coach from down the road.

Mr. Pierce looked at his list on the clipboard. 'Why Klara, of course,' he said, seeing he had almost forgotten her name written there. 'It's a good thing you made it in time,' whispered Mr. Pierce, running over to take her suitcase and ushering her aboard.

'How many times do we have to sing 'On Top of Spaghetti,'' said Sophie, the girl from detention class, in mid-conversation with Max and Chuck at the back row of the coach, the students of the class lifting their voices in raucous song. 'I mean the teachers haven't even told anyone to stop yet.'

'It's the spirit of the bus,' said Mr. Pierce, overhearing the conversation, making his way down to where the three were talking. The rest of the bus continued to sing. At that very moment one of them started with the first lines of 'Don't Stop Believing,' and quickly the bus started joining in.

'How are you guys doing back here?' he said to the three. 'Don't forget we're almost at the airport.'

'So remind me again about this Death Valley place?' said Sophie to Mr. Pierce, Mr. Pierce leaning in towards the three with his answer.

'Oh my, well, where to begin?' he said. 'It's near the border of Nevada and is the lowest, hottest and driest place in Northern America. It's a good job we're visiting in the spring right?'

'Chuck, that's a lot of M&M's you're taking with you,' said Max, watching Chuck pile the bags into his hamper from duty-free.

'Gotta be prepared for the journey you know,' said Chuck as they made their way around the shops at the airport.

The flight went smoothly from check-in, the students from Max's class boarding the plane one by one. Max watched as slowly they rose from the ground, the plane leaving the buildings and car parks into the distance as slowly the plane took flight.

All in all the flight went well, Max sitting back and resting, Chuck engrossed by his handheld console. Mr. Pierce had the habit of counting everyone, and then recounting for fear of leaving any of the students behind. Soon enough after five hours or so the plane landed smoothly in LAX.

It wasn't long before the class were all back on the coach again to drive to their hotel, before embarking on the trip to Death Valley the following day.

'Now guys, I don't know if you remember,' said Mr. Pierce, standing inside the bus once everyone had taken their seats, 'but this evening you are permitted to visit Saint Monica Pier which is close to where we'll be staying for the night, before our journey to Death Valley tomorrow. I don't know if you have heard of this pier already but it's a pretty famous one, dating back from 1909. There are plenty of rides and attractions there you can enjoy.'

The class cheered.

******

43

'Now Gentleman,' came the voice of a man, in what looked to be an abandoned warehouse. Three men stood there listening, the man speaking, turning away from a computer seated on a desk a few yards away from the rest of the three.

'Where is our $50,000?' said one of the men, standing on the left.

'My good sirs,' said the first man as he walked over to the three standing side by side. 'You'll get it in time. In fact you're due a lot more if you decide to continue working for me.'

'How much more?' said one of the men, slowly.

'What work?' said another.

'Well,' said the man pointing to what appeared to be a portable board covered by cloth. In one clean movement the man pulled off the cloth, the three men staring at what it was before them.

******

'Oh wow, they've got coffee and assortments,' said Chuck as they wheeled their luggage into the hotel room. 'And a pretty good HD TV too!' Chuck jumped onto the double bed, grabbing the remote and flicking on the channels. It wasn't long before Mr. Pierce was knocking on each door

44

counting the students. There was excitement in the air as doors opened and closed, students visiting each other from one room to the next.

'Remember guys, after dinner we'll all be heading down to St. Monica Pier,' shouted Mr. Pierce loudly. 'Meet you at the diner at 6.'

The evening sun set in the sky, music starting to play from nearby restaurants surrounding the hotel. Slowly the train of students left the hotel entrance, the smell of the sea nearby. 'I think that's everyone,' said Mr. Pierce quietly, the sky darkening. Mr. Pierce counted the students. 'All good,' he said. 'Now, it's just two blocks away,' he said, the class making their way to St. Monica Pier.

'Hey Max,' cried Chuck. 'They got a basketball game. See if you can get a stuffed toy for me. I've always wanted one of those Super Marios.'

'Alright,' said Max, dealing the games assistant two dollars.

There were screams as the sound of passengers on a nearby log-flume rocketed down the slope. 'You gotta get two out of three in the hoop,' exclaimed Chuck, standing behind Max, reading the rules on the nearby sign. Slowly Max picked up the basketball and sent the first soaring into the small hoop, a perfect swish. 'One more!' exclaimed

Chuck watching nervously. The ball flew into the air and just managed to squeeze through the hoop, bouncing on either side before dropping in.

'You did it!'

Chuck ran over to where the stuffed toys were pinned on the sideboard and grabbed one of the Marios.

The two walked around the pier, Chuck holding his new stuffed toy, Max eating on a stick of cotton candy he had just bought.

'Oh hey Max,' it was the voice of Sophie, with a couple of friends walking a different direction to the two boys. There were more screams from the nearby rollercoaster, some of the amusement park music being played, the sound of registers chiming from nearby kiosks.

It was then that it happened, and it seemed to happen out of nowhere. Max, Chuck and Sophie and her friends were talking when suddenly a great lurching sound from the rollercoaster shook the whole pier. People turned round and in screams watched on as the rollercoaster entering a loop-the-loop, lurched to a halt upside down, a great screeching sound coming from the track.

'Help!' screamed the passengers, the passengers hanging upside down. People around the pier started to point and cry. Max watched on, sensing a great panic filling the air.

46

Then suddenly a loud scream rang from one of the passengers. 'Help I'm slipping!' came the cry of a young girl.

It was Klara!

'Help I'm gonna fall!' came her cry once more, her screams becoming louder and more vivid. Without time to lose Max rushed forward through the crowd formed at the front of the rollercoaster.

'Hey Max, where are you going?' cried Sophie.

Klara screamed once more then slipped and fell through her seat. Then it happened within a flash. Max, within the midst of the crowd, pulled his hoodie over his head and instinctually jumped towards the hanging roller coaster where Klara appeared to be slipping. There was a loud scream. Max flew straight through the air, a good thirty feet or so before catching Klara, then out of view.

6

The sky was black from the nighttime as Max landed with a thud on the pier floorboards, Klara in his arms. Before she had time to think Max helped her onto her feet. The girl turned around to face Max, but Max, not wanting to reveal his identity, quickly ran off.

Stay for longer, thought Klara, the figure running down the pier.

What did I just do? Max thought, running down the pier behind the toilets where he was breathing and panting.

It wasn't long until the mechanic of the ride showed up. A good few minutes later the rollercoaster slunk down the track as slowly the mechanic and staff helped the terrified passengers off the ride. Eventually the police turned up too, and then the people of the media.

Klara turned, seeing the person run down the pier. 'Wait!' she cried. She watched as the figure ran off into the distance through the crowds. Slowly, she made her way back to the front of the rollercoaster where all the commotion was happening. Silently she snuck into the crowd where in-front of the rollercoaster policemen began quartering off the entrance to the ride, medics helping those in shock.

'Klara!' called Mr. Pierce from the crowd. Sifting his way through the people he grabbed Klara's arm. 'Stefanie says you were sitting with her on the ride? What happened?' he exclaimed.

'Someone… someone saved me,' she said, slowly.

'Now Klara, you take a big breather ok,' said Mr. Pierce once they had finally reached the hotel that night after medical checks and everything else. 'And you too Stefanie. Girls…' he said, 'if you have any problems, just know I'm only a few doors down the hall.'

There was a strange buzz going on about the hotel that night. Max lay there in his bed thinking about what he had done that evening. *Did Klara know that it was him who rescued her?*

'Wasn't that crazy?' said Chuck from his bed as he sat up and flicked on the side lamp. 'And to think that it was Stefanie and Klara were on the ride the whole time.'

******

The deafening sound of metal being cut rang inside the warehouse, sparks flying in all directions. The man behind the cutter stopped for a second looking at one of his men working at the desk where the television set was. 'Keep searching for those files,' he called across to the man. The other of his men was near to him drilling screws into place on the piece of machinery. They had been at it for over two hours now.

The man in charge was about to get back to work when suddenly he double-took, looking back at the television playing in the background on the desk. 'Wait,' he said pointing towards the man with the drill. 'Turn that off,' he said. The man stopped what he was doing. The man in charge fixed his eyes on the television set as he listened to the words of the newsreader.

'Strange scenes have been caught on footage today at St. Monica Pier in California. In what appeared to be a rollercoaster malfunctioning on a loop the loop - if it wasn't for a mysterious figure that supposedly 'flew in' and caught one of the girls who slipped from the roller coaster, it could very well have been the end for the young lady.' The newsreader's words were followed by footage caught from a phone by someone at the pier. The man watched on as he saw the roller coaster hanging upside down, people screaming as the camera focused in on the girl who appeared to be slipping from her seat. Then suddenly the strange image of a person wearing a hoodie, zipped up into the air catching the girl just in time as they flew together through the loop and out of view.

'What was that?' whispered the man in charge.

'Hey,' called the man. 'Rewind that,' he said.

Obeying, the other man picked up the remote and rewound the footage. It played through once more.

'Well, well, well,' said the man in charge, finally.

******

'And you're sure you're ok Klara?' said Mr. Pierce knocking on Stefanie and Klara's door the following morning. There was a buzz in the air, the Californian sun shining. People were still talking about what had happened last night with the rollercoaster and Klara.

'Now, it's going to take us a good five hours by coach to get to Death Valley,' said Mr. Pierce, once the hubbub had died down. 'I want you well rested before we get there, so make sure you get some extra sleep on the bus.'

The students put their suitcases into the side of the coach, Mr. Pierce counting each student as they boarded.

Max watched from his window, the coach passing through the city of Los Angeles and then towards the deserts of California where nothing but desert hills and plains were.

It took exactly five hours, slowly the bus coming to a halt.

'Well kids,' said Mr. Pierce loudly from the front of the bus. 'Looks like we made it.'

Chuck yawned and stretched as Max nudged him from his sleep. 'Wait— what?' he said, waking up, stretching, his beanie pillow falling from the side of his seat.

'Oh wow!' exclaimed Chuck as he looked through the window. Chuck gazed at his surroundings as they got out of

51

the bus, taking in the environment, a warm wind passing by.

'We're here folks!' said Mr. Pierce excitedly, the bus driver beginning to help the students get their suitcases out in the heat of the afternoon.

The students made their way to their hotel in high spirits, passing the pools and the water fountains by the entrance of the hotel.

'It's so hot,' exclaimed Chuck, the group beginning to check-in at the hotel reception.

The following morning Mr. Pierce was at the students' doors making sure everyone was up in time for the morning tour of the valley. 'We'll be 282 feet below sea level, in Badwater Basin,' he cried. 'There we'll measure the salt levels!'

After another much quicker coach ride, the students slowly made their way out of the bus. What surrounded Max amazed him. There in the distance lay a long line of hills covering the horizon of a vast and spectacular plain. The most amazing part of it all though thought Max was the glistening of the white salt that sparkled from the desert floor. It lay there still in the distance, the sun shining off it from where they were standing in the car park. Together the class made their way onto a wooden boardwalk pathway which went over the desert floor. A small, wooden sign read 'Badwater Basin 252 ft / 85.5 metres below sea level.'

'There's nothing here…' said Chuck, looking out into the distance.

'That's kind of the point,' joked Max as they made their way across the wooden path and over to where the salt was laying.

The next few days in Death Valley went by smoothly. Mr. Pierce could be seen here and there helping with students making measurements of the salt. He looked on proudly, the class listening contently to the tour guide. He even let the class go swimming in the hotel pools, having their own leisure time during lunch and in the evenings. Soon enough the time came for them to take the long journey back to LA.

'Look what I got,' said Chuck as they boarded the bus, holding up a small tube of valley salt he had bought from the visitors' centre.

'Cool,' said Max.

It wasn't long before they were on the road again. However, about fifteen minutes in, one of Max's classmates already needed a restroom break.

'Alright folks,' said Mr. Pierce, 'looks like we've got a ten-minute break already. Do what you need to do, get some snacks and be back at the coach in ten.'

The students began to line up to buy their goodies at the gas station, Max joining the line at the end. Soon enough ten minutes had passed and all the students were back on the coach. It was just Max left at the counter buying some Cheetos.

'Max, we're waiting for you,' called Mr. Pierce, Max making his way over to where the bus was standing. It was a hot day and there was a warm wind that passed through the gas station. Mr. Pierce looked up at the sky as he felt the heat against his skin. There in the distance looked to be a small plane in the horizon by the desert hills. It swerved in the sky as Mr. Pierce watched it glide along into the distance. 'Must be military,' mumbled Mr. Pierce.

'Max, we don't have all day,' called Mr. Pierce from the bus.

'Coming,' called Max running over to the coach. The sound of the jet grew louder and louder, Mr. Pierce looking up, the black jet thing swooping down from the sky, diving down towards where they were standing.

'Max!?' said Mr. Pierce suddenly, the piercing sound of the jet filling the desert plain. In one clean movement it swooped downwards, picking up Max, like a bird with its prey, zooming past the intersection of the gas station. Soaring in the air, it swerved then flew out into the distance. 'Max!' shouted Mr. Piers.

'Let go of me!' cried Max flying through the air. He felt tough arms grip his body tightly. *Who was it that was holding him?* It wasn't a plane or a jet, because whatever it was that was carrying him was too small to be that. 'What do you want with me?' cried Max as he soared through the air, the sound of engines above him.

The jet-like thing flew back down the road, the way the coach came, past the hotels, soaring back over Badwater Basin and towards the hills.

'Say goodbye kid,' came a voice from above. The jet began to soar upwards and into the sky, the altitude increasing every second, the pair flying over Badwater Basin.

Max, anticipating what the person was going to do, felt the release of the man's arms. Max would have fallen from the sky there and then if it wasn't for Max's quick reactions. Instinctively Max grabbed the man's free arm and hung on for dear life just moments after the man had released him. Gripping tightly he tilted the trajectory of the flying jet-like plane downwards. Together Max and the man began to spiral. Down they flew, the ground becoming nearer every second. Letting go just in time Max dropped to the ground tumbling and rolling across the desert plain. Stopping himself he looked on as the man crashed into the ground, skidding across the desert floor with what appeared to be a big engine like jetpack strapped to his back. The man slid across the ground, the back of the jetpack sliding across the ground, the man still strapped to it. When it came to a halt, quickly the man undid the harness and stumbling out of the jetpack got his balance once more.

'You!' he cried at last, his eyesight on Max. Instinctively Max started to run, running back towards where the Badwater Basin visitor centre was.

The man behind tried to run too, but hobbling, realising he couldn't.

'Agh,' cried the man in pain, Max running into the visitor centre where a few officials were already starting to come out onto the boardwalk to see what had happened.

'What in tarnation is going on?' Mr. Pierce shouted as the school coach came to a halt outside Badwater Basin Visitor Centre. Max stood there by the entrance looking all dirty, salt and dirt over his t-shirt and jeans. Mr. Pierce from the bus beckoned Max to come over, Max by the reception, with a few visitor centre officials surrounding him.

'Are you alright Max?' Mr. Pierce said finally as Max stepped onto the bus, his t-shirt and pants still covered in salt and dirt.

'This boy has just witnessed a flying vehicle crash land onto the basin,' came an official, who was attempting to talk to Mr. Pierce.

Max felt dishevelled, but kept quiet. The journey back to LAX airport seemed so long. Questions began to run through his head. *What had just happened to him? What did that man in the strange jet-pack device want with him? Was it something to do with his new abilities?* Max continued to stay quiet, Chuck entertained by his games, hardly seeming to have noticed anything. 'Want some M&M's?' he said, offering Max a handful on the bus.

******

'You sure you're ok boss?' said the driver, turning round to the man sitting in the back of a van.

'I'm ok… honestly,' said the man grimacing. He put a hand on the side of his leg. 'No,' he said finally, 'nothing broken, just…' There was a slight grimace in his eyes.

7

'Did you have a good time?' called Jenny from the roadside, slowly the school coach coming to a halt. Max reached for his suitcase, out popping Mr. Pierce from the bus, helping Max grab his things. 'Well did you guys have a good time?' said Jenny as Max followed by Mr. Pierce made their way up the drive of the Fritz' household. Mr. Pierce appeared nervous.

'Well goodbye then,' said Mr. Pierce, looking at Max and then to his mum anxiously.

'Goodbye Mr. Pierce,' said Jenny.

'So Honey,' said Mrs Fritz, helping Max inside with his luggage. 'Did you have a good time?' she said, watching Max slowly make his way upstairs. Max closed the door behind him. 'Is something alright?' came the voice of the mother from outside the door.

Max took a few seconds to answer. 'No everything's alright,' he said. 'Guess I'm a bit tired from the journey, that's all.'

'Alright Honey,' said the mum. 'Just call me if you need anything. Oh I'm so glad you're back home. I've missed you Max,' she said.

Later that night Max sat at his desk and switched on his desktop computer. Still feeling shaken from what had happened at Badwater Basin, Max googled the news, typing in 'St. Monica Pier.' Surely enough there were articles about the recent roller coaster malfunction, even YouTube videos showing the same clip of a blurry figure in the distance jumping up and catching the falling passenger. Quickly Max switched to news for Death Valley. Low and behold there were already news articles circulating regarding what had happened. 'Strange flying object crash lands in Badwater Basin,' read the local California news article. There was also video footage showing the aftermath of the crash. Max leaned in closer seeing that the flying device did indeed look like a type of large jetpack. Except there was no footage of the mysterious man, just the wreckage of the jetpack on the desert floor. He shut down his computer and sat there, staring at his desk. *What should he do next?* he thought as he grabbed a pen and began to scribble down some notes on his sticky pad. *Would he tell people what really happened?* he wondered. *And should he tell people about his new ability?*

******

The front door to a wooden, two-storey detached house opened, sat in the suburbs of Chicago. Out stepped a petite fifteen-year-old girl onto the wooden decking of her home, the red sun beginning to sink in the sky, the girl looking further down the road to where the horizon of the Chicago city scrapers met with the melting sun. 'Isn't it beautiful?' came the sound of the mother's voice from behind her. Klara smiled and turned around. Hanging around the girl's neck was a DSLR camera. 'Why don't you take a picture?' said the mum.

'It's alright,' said Klara.

'What's up princess?' said the mother, questioning.

'Oh nothing much really… I'm ok,' she said.

Her mum gave Klara a big hug, the sound of the birds cooing in the evening sun. Then quietly the mother left the decking, closing the front door behind her.

There stood Klara alone, leaning against the patio fence breathing heavy sighs. It had been exactly two days since she had been rescued.

'Where are you?' she whispered as a cool evening breeze passed by.

******

'Hey Chuck,' said Max, one of the following days at school. They were back in the diner and Chuck had helped himself to two scoops of vanilla ice-cream.

'Uhuh?' said Chuck, watching one of his favourite animes on his phone screen, scooping the ice-cream into his mouth.

'Chuck if I told you I had the ability to jump, would you believe me?'

'Max, everyone knows you're good at basketball,' said Chuck with a mouthful of ice cream.

'But it's more than that…' said Max.

'Oh, so you wanna go pro?' said Chuck looking up at Max briefly. 'I thought you were focusing more on your Taekwondo.'

'No…' said Max slowly, 'it's just…' Then Max stopped speaking. It would be too ridiculous for anyone to believe right now. Chuck would start thinking he had gone crazy, and even if Chuck was to witness Max's amazing, new jumping ability, things might get out of hand. *He would get so much attention from school... Who knows what might happen next? Fame?* This wasn't exactly what Max wanted. As the end of the term drew near, Max still had some questions in the back of his mind. *Who was the man in the jetpack? What did he want with him?* wondered Max.

Today was Max's final Taekwondo lesson of the term. Max sweated putting every ounce of energy into his Taekwondo routines.

That afternoon after his class had finished Max ran into Chicago City Centre. He ran to Lincoln Park and began to jump through the trees and in the opening of the park. He ran and ran, through Lincoln park and back through the suburbs towards his home. Passing his house he continued to run, taking the bus towards a park called 'Mortom Arboretum,' west of his home, a place with open fields surrounded by trees. He began to practise his jumping there too. Here there were less people likely to spot him, gliding and soaring through the air.

The holidays had begun, but Max still didn't quite feel himself. He still couldn't stop thinking about the man that had nearly killed him at Death Valley. *Like a bird of prey he had stalked him and caught him in the desert. And where on earth did he get that jetpack-like device from? What did he want with him?*

For the most part the spring holidays went well. Max invited Chuck around to his house a few times. At home, Max studied in his room when he could, reading and playing video games. Anytime he did go outside, he dedicated to jumping and running.

That night, three days before school was to start again, Max dreamt a strange dream. He dreamt he was back in the same shopping mall he had been in when he had seen the crime in the jewellery store. The eyes of the robber haunted him as the robber looked this way and that, scanning the store for anyone who might make any sudden moves. The robber had someone held hostage, like they do in the movies, except the person he held was his mother! Her beige hair was recognizable from a mile off. 'Make any sudden moves and I'll shoot!' he said, the look of fear in his mothers eyes as his hand covered her mouth. Then there in the store, another assistant who was behind the jewellery counter slowly reached for the glass cabinet, opening it, his hands shaking, handing the jewels to the man. It was his father!

Max woke up in a haze of sweat. He looked around him, sensing if everything was ok. All was normal there in the dark of his bedroom. 'Mum?' he said softly. 'Dad?'

The following morning Max had his breakfast his mum had prepared for him. 'This tastes good mum,' he said, still thinking over the dream in his mind.

'Oh great Honey,' said the mum, washing the dishes.

'Did you want me to take the trash out on my way out?' Max said, putting his plate and cup in the dishwasher.

'That would be great Honey,' said Jenny.

Max took the bus into Chicago City Centre. He found he still couldn't stop thinking about the dream. He decided he would spend some time visiting his favourite sport shops and look at all his favourite sneakers, maybe have a bite to eat at Luigi's pizza parlour and just relax. It might shake off the strange feeling he had gotten from the dream last night.

After visiting Luigi and his pizza parlour, Max holding a cup of soda walked down the pavement and towards the bus stop ready to go home. Just before he had reached the stop, he saw his bus pulling in to collect more passengers. Quickly Max started to run over to where the bus was in an attempt to board it just in time. Just as he had started running, within a flash he crashed into someone who was just coming out of a shop from the high street. Bumping into her by accident she nearly fell to the ground, holding a bag full of items which spilled out onto the sidewalk. 'Oh my,' she exclaimed. 'Did I make you miss your bus?'

The girl was Klara.

'No no, it's alright. I'll get the next one,' said Max. He helped Klara get up and began retrieving what had spilled out of her bag. They were paintbrushes and a brand new sketchbook.

'I didn't know you liked art?' said Max as he handed her back the couple of brushes and the sketchbook that had fallen, the papers turning in the wind.

'I'm a photographer too,' she smiled as she pointed to her DSLR camera that was hanging around her neck. 'What are you doing out here in the city centre?' she said as they began to walk towards Max's bus stop.

'Listen,' said Max finally, once they had arrived at the stop. 'Did you want to get a drink at Juice Bar?' said Max, seizing the opportunity. 'I feel like I owe you one.'

'Sure,' said Klara.

That afternoon Klara spent a good ninety minutes talking with Max in Juice Bar, further into the city centre. Max smiled, knowing he had saved Klara at St. Monica Pier, and yet she had no idea of it herself. 'And you still don't know who or what it was that caught you that night on the pier?' asked Max.

'No,' said Klara, taking a sip from her smoothie. 'Isn't it weird?' she said.

'What type of art do you do?' asked Max, as their conversation drew to a close.

'Oh mainly sketches. I love still life,' she said, showing some pictures of her drawings and paintings of different types of flowers and fruit from her phone.

Max was amazed at the quality of her art. 'And you really did all that yourself?' he asked as they got up from the table.

'Hey Max, what have you been up to today?' called Jenny from the kitchen hearing Max open the front door.

'Oh nothing much Mum,' said Max, making his way over to where his mum was doing the dishes. 'Well actually, I met someone from school.'

'Oh and who was that?' asked the mum, curiously.

'Oh just a girl called Klara. She's new. I mean she started last term.'

'Well that's great,' said Mum. 'Did you offer her a drink or something? Were you nice to her?'

'Of course,' said Max, 'it wasn't arranged or anything. I met her outside Luigi's Pizza by accident. She was just leaving an art shop.'

'An art shop eh?' said the mum.

'She's great at it, you know. She showed me her drawings.'

'Great,' said Jenny.

Despite the afternoon going well for Max, that night things didn't go so smoothly. Max kept having the same dream he had the night before, at the jewellery store. It troubled him as he tossed and turned in bed. He thought of all the crimes that could be happening within the city of Chicago right now. And who knows who it might involve. Innocent lives caught up in the midst of it all, like the way his mother and father were held hostage in his dream.

Max woke up in a cold sweat.

8

The following day was the beginning of Max's third term of school. 'Alright Max, up and at 'em,' said Jenny, knocking on the door. Strangely Max still couldn't stop thinking about the dream he had experienced the past couple of nights. He thought of it in registration, in maths class, and in biology.

'Max are you sure you're alright?' said one of the teachers during IT class. Max was staring blankly into nothing, as the rest of the students were busy doing their tasks on the computers.

'Hey Max,' said Chuck at the diner later that afternoon, 'Did you hear there's going to be a homecoming ceremony for our class at the end of term?'

'Oh right,' said Max.

'Yeah,' said Chuck. 'I checked all the rules. Anyone in our class can be nominated before the final ballot a week before the end of term. There's going to be a Homecoming King and Queen you know. I just hope the voting is fair,' added Chuck.

******

'So what's next Boss?' said one of the men in the warehouse. Turning on the TV, he sat onto the office chair, spinning his legs up onto the desk. 'It took us how many weeks to get your engine finished and we go crash it on the first day? Is there a change of plan? I mean maybe we could work on our longevity,' joked the man.

The boss was lost in thought as he walked up and down the warehouse, partially listening in to what his employees were saying, partially thinking about what needed to be done.

'That boy needs to go,' said the man finally.

They turned and looked at him.

'Boss, what exactly has he done to you?' said one of his employees.

'I just... don't like him,' said the boss as he shook his head. Makes me think he'll interfere with what we gotta do, you know... He's got to go...' said the boss finally. 'And we've gotta start over and come back stronger... We'll need a new set of wings.'

******

68

Klara made her way out of the art studio at school. 'I'm gonna have to go get an extra supply of red paint,' said Klara, looking back at her art teacher.

'Ok thanks Klara,' said the teacher, looking concerned. 'I could have sworn I had extra red somewhere, I guess it's all gone.'

Klara made her way through the empty corridors of the school. It wasn't until she was coming back from the supply cupboard that she saw Max again in the corridor. They talked for a few moments.

If it wasn't the bell ringing for the end of the lesson Max might have forgotten they were still in conversation and still at school.

'Hey Klara?' he said, seizing the opportunity, 'Did you want to get another drink?' he said, 'I mean… at Juice Bar again, say 4 o'clock today?'

'Sure,' said Klara, the corridors filling up with people.

That afternoon Max and Klara met again at Juice Bar, the pair ordering mango smoothies. Max sat down with Klara. They talked and talked. When they had finished slurping up their smoothies, it was time to go. 'I enjoyed my time here,' she said looking at Max, Max opening the door.

'Me too,' said Max.

Klara, like candy, had left a good taste in Max's mouth. Max couldn't stop thinking about her on the way home. The thought of Klara made Max feel good. Yet strangely he could never really stop thinking about his dream he had endured the past couple of nights either, his father and mother in the jewellery store, and as the time came for him to go to bed, even the thought of Klara could not dispel his worry and sense of fear.

He had made his mind up. He sat there in his room on his personal computer browsing the news, looking at different articles online of both sport and regular. Tomorrow things would change.

The following day Max anticipated the end of each lesson by staring at the clock as the time slowly ticked by. Chuck played on his handheld console at the diner at lunch. Max kept silent as he let Chuck get lost in his games.

That night, Max in his bedroom, slipped on his best running shoes, putting on a dark hoodie and some black jogging pants. Adjusting his glasses, quietly he opened the window of his bedroom, the bedroom directly above his dad's garage. Quietly, he slipped out onto the garage roof, climbing down to the ground.

The city was quieter than during the day, the city grounds kept illuminated by the artificial light as the night sky lingered on. Max saw the nightlife, people spilling out of clubs, the quieter roads, the taxis that worked the late hours. He walked along the Chicago River as it flowed calmly through the inner city. A couple hours passed and Max could not find anyone or anything causing trouble. Max began to wonder if what he was doing was too ridiculous. It wasn't until Max had almost decided to go home that it happened.

Max made his way down an empty street to the nearest bus stop to return home, when he saw a man from across the street huddled close to the door of what appeared to be a bakery, the front windows showing empty spaces for cakes and bread to be displayed. At the back of the store Max could see the counter and the stools where people could take a seat. Max watched from across the road hiding behind the bus stop seeing the man continuing to knock on the front door of the bakery. Half of the lights of the shop were still on, a woman from the bakery walking towards the door, the man continuing to knock.

'I'm sorry we're closed,' came a small voice from across the road as Max listened in. The woman opened the door slightly to let the man know. That was her first mistake, Max watching on in horror, the man gripping open the door just as she had tried to shut it, sending it flying back, the woman falling to the floor.

'Listen sir, we are closed,' came her troubled voice from the ground. 'I am going to have to call the police.'

'Unload the register,' came the voice of the man.

Max watched on in horror as he saw the man pull out a small firearm, pointing it in her direction briefly. This was too much for Max, he had to intervene, and so as stealthily as possible he ran across the street, over to the back of the man and without him realising, poked him on the back. In a flash the man turned round Max instinctually sending out a soaring punch, the man ducking just in time. The man pulled out his firearm pointing it directly at Max. Without any time to waste Max jumped up and kicked it out of his hand, the gun flying off somewhere to the side of the road. It was then that the brawl began, the two men swinging punches left and right, Max ducking for every punch the man tried to send at him. At last Max sent the man a powerful right kick to the side of his body sending him flying diagonally, crashing into the middle of the road. Before the man had time to clamber to his feet, Max quickly scoured the sidewalk for the firearm that had fallen out of the man's hand.

Quickly he picked it up, Max pointing it at the thief who got to his feet. The man waited in fear... then in a flash ran off. For a few seconds Max continued to hold out the firearm, the man running away.

'And don't come back again!' Max shouted.

Then turning to the woman who was watching, he said, 'I'm sorry this had to happen ma'am' said Max, shaken a little himself, the baker still in shock.

'Well thank you sir,' the woman said finally, having gotten up from the floor, 'but I'm afraid I'm still going to have to ring the police.'

'Understood ma'am,' said Max, dropping the weapon.

Then Max ran off.

Quietly Max climbed up the garage and snuck back into his room, his window he had already left a touch open. Max's heartbeat was racing. His first night out on the streets of Chicago was kind of a success. Max changed his clothes, then went to bed.

******

That night the Chicago Police Department was alive with people doing their night shifts.

'Look at this, guys,' said one of the junior policemen watching the fight caught by a CCTV camera on the street by the side of 'Ms Silva's Fine Bakery.'

'Look at him go,' whispered the policeman beckoning to some of his other colleagues as they crowded around the monitor. Little did they know there was a greater presence behind them, the deputy chief watching on too, the boy on the screen fighting the man out on the road until at last his kick sent the man flying to the ground. 'Where did this guy come from?' said the junior policeman. The deputy chief watched on, the junior unknowing, rewinding and playing the tape back.

******

There was something about last night's events that made Max feel proud of himself. Max making his way to school, replayed last night's fight at the bakery in his mind. The punching, the kicking, it all made Max feel empowered. He felt like he could take on anything.

'Hey Max, today is the day for homecoming nominations. Cool eh?' said Chuck as they met outside the gates of their school.

That day Max could only think of getting out into the city once more. To put right what was wrong, to help stop the crime. The lessons passed in a blur, the homecoming nominations he didn't care about. Although he did hear a few classmates were already spreading around Klara's name as a possible contender.

9

That night in his bedroom, Max changed his clothes putting on the same outfit he had worn last night. Quietly he slipped out of the window and ran down the road towards where the bus stop was.

Max scoured the city, walking unobtrusively around the intersections, the South Loop, the Near West Side, all the places where Max thought something fishy might be happening. In fact it was only about thirty minutes in that Max caught his first crime of the night. He saw a man walk down the road and sensing something strange coming from him, Max crossed the road and made his way behind him. The man seemed to have his eye on a woman just further along the sidewalk. It was clear that they didn't know each other, yet it was the strange way in which the man kept his eyes on the woman's bag that made Max notice.

Quietly Max followed the man down the street, never letting him know he was there. Max was certain he knew what the man was about to do.

75

Seizing his opportunity the man ran over to the woman walking unaware down the road. The man pounced on her and before she had any time to think, the man ripped off her bag, unslinging it roughly from her body. The woman called out in desperation as the man ran off. 'Hey, that's mine!' she shouted.

In a flash Max started running towards the man, realising the only way he could catch him was to jump towards him. And so he did, at full speed, darting through the air landing just behind him.

'Hey you!' called out Max, landing about two feet behind the thief. The man turned around as Max tackled him to the floor, the man dropping the bag upon impact. Pinning him down the man struggled to break free from Max's grip. The woman, just in time, ran over to get her bag as Max continued to hold the thief.

'Go!' he cried.

The woman obeyed Max, looking back at him, thanking him and dashing off into the city.

Max, letting the man get to his feet… jeered at him. 'Not so bad now are ya?' laughed Max.

The man struck out at Max, but Max dodging his punch, kicked the man sending him flying backwards onto the road. The man feeling the blow scrambled to his feet, Max approaching him. The man sensing Max was more dangerous than he had ever anticipated turned and ran the opposite direction.

'And don't let me see you near that young lady again—' called out Max as he watched the man disappear the opposite way of the woman.

The night continued to be a successful one for Max. Leaving the scene of the crime he jumped through the dark of the streets avoiding anyone that might see him. By the time another hour had passed Max was also successful in stopping a man stealing a car. It happened at about 2.30am in the morning when Max passing a small road saw a man hidden in the dark of the street attempting to pull a car door open with a crowbar. Just as the man opened it, the alarm went off, Max running over to where the thief was. In the nick of time the thief managed to jump in and swerve the car around, driving down the road.

Max, certain he could catch the car, took a big run up as fast as he could and jumped into the air landing directly on top of the bonnet. The man swerved the car as Max held on tight.

Climbing around the car Max opened the side door, the man driving faster and faster in full panic mode. Max kicked him senseless as he entered through the side, the car slowly coming to a stop as Max reached for the steering wheel. The man lay in the driver's seat unconscious, Max, grabbing his phone from his pocket, calling 911.

Max looked around for the nearest road sign exclaiming — 'there's been a car theft on Friars Street. Come quickly!' he said, putting down the phone, not giving enough time for the person on the other end to reply.

It was well into the night now and soon enough Max began to feel tired. Soaring through the streets at night, he jumped and ran, making his way home, landing directly at the foot of his garage. Max climbed up the side of the building and slid through the window into his room.

The long summer holiday term continued, the days getting hotter as each day passed. Max, deciding that he couldn't just go out and help the city of Chicago every night, limited his 'night sessions.' In fact Max nearly forgot about them after a week had passed, yet it was as if the mere acts of going out and helping the city had dispelled any fear of the nightmares that had bothered him recently.

10

'Chuck, raise the fairy lights a little higher,' called out Mrs. Stone, the art teacher as she scanned the sports hall where the homecoming celebration was to be. 'These decorations have got to be perfect,' she called out, the class following her every instruction.

'Bring down the disco ball a little further,' she said, Max on the stepladder, loosening the chain in which the disco ball was hanging from. There in the corner of the room was Klara, spraying trophies she had made earlier, the colour of gold, one for the homecoming king and the other for the queen.

Soon enough the day of the homecoming came. Each student was to dress smartly for the event. Klara, one of the nominees for homecoming queen, waited onstage nervously with two other girls from her Freshman year, her white dress sparkling under the stage lights, the crowd cheering louder and louder inside the sports hall. Together the three girls held hands as the music blared out from the stage speakers.

'Now,' said Mr. Pierce, the proms host, over the microphone, dressed in suit and bowtie. 'I want you all to give a warm round of applause for our top three queens. These three girls represent our school and deserve the best reception we can give them.'

There was a whoop and holler as the three girls smiled on stage.

'Now time for the result. Our homecoming queen is…'

The three girls' names were thrown about the hall as the freshman class cheered and shouted their favourite to win.

'Klara!' came the voice of Mr. Pierce at last, as cheers erupted, the music blaring. There were a few moments of celebration, as Klara walked forward and received her crown as well as the trophy she had made earlier. The sound of cheering died down again as moments of anticipation kicked in once more. 'And now… our homecoming king is… … … Jake Harris!'

Klara made her way through the crowds of the sports hall and out the side door where the sunset rested over the suburbs of Chicago. There in the 'Science Garden,' with its view over the track and field and next to the sports hall stood Klara sipping on some lemonade she had taken from the bar. The evening was a hot one as the red evening sky warmed the horizon, the fairy lights already turned on around the veranda. Everyone was still inside dancing to the music, but Klara, in her white dress, stayed outside. She took a deep sigh, as she wondered where on earth her rescuer was. *It's been how many weeks already, and still you don't tell me who or where you are?* she thought, the music from the hall turning slow, different couples joining together, the music playing on.

Just then, a small figure in the distance came into view, a boy running closer to the sports hall. He could be seen making his way past the track and field towards where Klara was, jogging, making his way over to the veranda. It was Max!

Spotting Klara standing outside, Max made his way over to where she was. 'Did I miss anything?' he asked as the slow rendition of 'Unchained Melody' began to play in the background.

'Not really,' said Klara. She smiled as Max looked around, wearing a blue bow tie and black and white suit.

'Wanna dance?' said Klara finally as she took the last sip of her lemonade.

'Sure,' said Max, slowly Max resting his hands on Klara, out in the veranda, the fairy lights beginning to glow in the evening sky.

'Why are you so late?' asked Klara finally, smiling at Max as they continued to sway to the music.

'To be honest,' said Max at long last, 'I forgot. I was busy—'

'It's ok,' said Klara, 'you didn't miss much.'

The slow music played on, each lyric of 'Unchained Melody' filling the air.

11

It was the beginning of the summer holidays and each and every student of Chicago High was excited for the break that was coming their way. The first few days Max and Chuck were found down the arcade, shooting zombies, racing virtual motorbikes down freeways and sipping on cola and slush puppies.

But further down the suburbs of Chicago things were a different story. At the abandoned warehouse the four men worked and worked on their new project, one man by the desk with the security cameras, the other guarding out front and finally the boss and the fourth man on the main project itself.

'The jet needs bigger engines this time,' said the boss, visualising the wings. 'It needs more 'oomph,' I'm thinking close to 300mph. What do you say?' said the boss, turning to his employee.

The days of summer passed. Max, almost forgetting about his 'night sessions' entirely began to enjoy the summer holidays as much as he could. He spent most of his time focusing on video games, his Taekwondo, playing basketball with friends, and reading. Soon enough there were talks of a summer parade which got most of the town excited, Max included. As for Klara, Klara continued to meet up with Max during the summer weeks. Max, interested in Klara's art, planned to see a youth exhibition that was on at the townhall, featuring Klara's work. Max was impressed by the still life, the fruits, the oranges, the vases and the flowers. Anything put on a table, Klara could paint it.

******

The four men continued their work, the jetpacks' day of completion arriving. But as they worked, it occurred to the boss that something must be done about the boy. Strangely the boss had almost forgotten about him during the time they were reconstructing their second jetpack. But deep down the boss knew the problem had to be tackled. The man thought it through, thinking up a way he could eliminate the boy once and for all.

******

Soon enough it was the day of the parade. 'Chicago's Downtown Summer Parade' would be taking place on the same road that passed the townhall and would be lasting for an entire hour. Klara watched from the window, the parade passing the front doors of the town hall, where she was sitting by her paintings. The exhibition she had promised to attend for three days straight, one of the days clashing with the parade. The music blared as the different acts in costumes, marched on, balloons and floats passing by.

'Hey Max,' called Chuck as they pushed their way to the front of the crowd by the side of the street. 'You get a good view from here,' he said, eating some candy floss off a stick. So far Max was impressed by the parade, the different people waving to and fro, from the floats.

'Oh Chuck' exclaimed Max, suddenly. Chuck turned around.

'I just realised I gotta be at Klara's gallery. Guess I double booked,' he said.

Chuck nodded. Max made his way round the back of the parade, crossed the street and over to where the town hall was. Entering Max could see Klara's paintings just a few rows down the exhibition aisle. Klara sat on the stool as she talked to the few passers-by that were in the exhibition rather than the parade.

'You're missing a good time out there,' joked Max as he came towards Klara.

Klara laughed.

There was a sudden shudder of the ground, the sound of an explosion going off nearby. The two froze. Soon enough screams could be heard from outside.

'What was that?' whispered Klara, her face growing paler. Klara rushed towards the entrance of the town hall and looked outside. She could see people from the parade stopping what they were doing, people beginning to run down the road. She turned around looking for Max.

'Max?' she called, looking down the exhibition aisle. He was nowhere in site.

Max opened up the backdoor of the town hall, clambering out onto the back lane, the sound of screaming coming from the main road in which the parade was on. Running down the side lane of the town hall and to the front of the street he quickly mixed himself into the running crowd, looking around trying to pinpoint exactly where the explosion had come from. People were running, like the flow of a river down the road. Max guessed the explosion had come from the secluded garden at the clock tower further up, people running from that direction. He kept his eyes towards the clock tower, people running faster and faster, the panic and buzz lifting. Max made his way as close to the clock tower as he could where the secluded garden was, sifting through the people. Another explosion went off, and practically in the same spot as before! And then he began to see it, a massive truck flipping and flying towards him like something out of a movie or a game, flipping and toppling over as it tumbled towards the people. There were gasps and screams, people running this way and that, yet Max stood in the midst of the street, bracing for impact, obstructing the toppling truck before it had any possibility of crashing into anyone who was in the way. Max stood there on the street alone... holding back the truck!

Soon enough there were cheers from all around once the crowd realised what Max had done, but they didn't last long as a very loud, strange alarm went off nearby, mixing in with the car alarms that were already blaring. There were police and journalists running to the side of the roads, some already parked close to where a view of the truck was, and Max. Journalists spoke into cameras, photographers took pictures.

Max followed the sound of the strange alarm. He didn't like the sound of it at all, the sound coming from the town hall. There was no sight of anyone inside as he made his way in, everyone seemingly fled the building, including Klara.

There in the corner of the room stood what appeared to be a strange box with a lever on it. It was where the sound of the alarm was coming from, but the strangest of kinds, all distorted and menacing sounding.

Does this mean another detonation? thought Max as he ran over to the strange box that looked to be like a pile of explosives in the corner. The alarm blared from it with what Max saw to be a digital timer. There were only twenty seconds left on the clock! Max looked around him as he called out. 'Look, I think there's another bomb here. Help, I think there's another bomb!' But everyone had fled the scene. He placed his hand on the red handle, not daring to push it. He looked around the box wondering if something could be diffused. Just then what appeared to be a journalist ran into the room with a camera hanging around his neck. He appeared to be looking for any opportunity for a photo, it being evident that he had heard the strange alarm too. Within a split second he put his finger on his camera taking a picture of Max there by the box, Max's hands on it. In a split second, the flash of the camera went off, Max turning around, the flash blinding him. And just like that the journalist ran out of the town hall again.

Then another explosion happened… Max felt the earth shudder all around him as he looked up. What came next horrified Max as he began to see the ceiling of the town hall breaking up, falling into bits. The walls of the town hall rumbling and shaking as Max watched on in horror as bricks and tiles and wood from the ceiling started to fall from above.

Max heard the muffled sounds of people calling above him. It was pitch black and when he tried to move, he couldn't. Max struggled to breathe as the voices above him grew louder, dust covering his face, his heart beating wildly. It was only until the final brick above him was moved, that he could see the blue sky once more. The voices above him grew stronger.

'I think we got one over here sir.'

The final brick was removed, Max seeing a hand reach towards him. 'It's ok buddy,' came the voice, Max grabbing an arm as he was lifted out. Handed a bottle of water Max was taken to a nearby medical bus where he was given a check up. Despite a few bruises here and there Max was in remarkably good shape.

12

'Hey Max,' said Chuck swinging his portable game remote around the place. 'We've got to get to the final boss of this level. Don't screw up,' he said.

'I won't,' said Max, the pair working together.

There was a knock at the door.

'Mum I'll get it,' called Max as he paused the game. Chuck was waiting, anticipating finishing the level. Max opened the front door.

There stood three policemen looking very serious. One of them spoke.

'May we speak to your parents,' he said.

'I'll just go get them,' said Max.

Max returned with his mum and dad and went back to the video game with Chuck.

'What!?' shrieked Jenny from the doorway a couple of moments into their conversation.

'Yes ma'am,' said the first policeman. Max continued to play the game with Chuck, yet as they played Max tried to listen to every word his parents and the policemen were saying.

'I'm sorry, but Max has done what?' said the father finally.

The policemen stepped inside and made their way over to where Max was by the TV. Max could sense the policemen standing behind him.

'Max,' said one of the policemen.

Max turned around.

'I'm sorry but you can't!' cried Max's mum as the policeman shut the door to the police car, Max sitting inside handcuffed. The two policemen made their way back to where Max's mum and dad were standing out in the front garden.

'For the near future, I'm afraid Max will have to be detained. We still have some more evidence to file through, but right now we can't risk Max roaming the city any longer. I'm sorry ma'am.'

Jenny hung her head. Max looked through the darkened window of the car. Seeing his mother look sad made him feel horrible inside. *What had he done?* he wondered. *Maybe the game was up, maybe it was time to tell others about his ability. And yet he had done nothing wrong?* As the two policemen outside got back into the car Max turned around seeing his mother begin to cry on her father's shoulder, slowly the police car drove away.

The door was locked, Max slumping to the ground of the temporary youth prison cell. He felt terrible inside waiting for something to happen, for someone to come let him out, yet two hours had passed and still nothing. Eventually Max fell asleep there on the bed.

The sound of a key in the door woke Max, the heavy door to his prison cell opening. There were the familiar three policemen and what appeared to be a detective standing at the front door. They ushered Max out and into a private room where Max took a seat. Sat opposite, the detective pulled out a tablet from his bag. Switching it on he put it on the table in front of Max.

'Yesterday, at 12.36pm an explosion went off by the clock tower in downtown Chicago. What happened next, well…' The man showed Max the tablet. There Max watched the footage, someone who had captured it with a phone seemed to have caught the whole event, the truck flipping towards Max, Max out there on the street embracing for impact.

'I've also got this,' said the detective. He turned off the tablet and swapped it for a photograph. There in the photograph was Max knelt by a box of 'explosives' in the corner of the town hall, Max's hand over the red lever.

'Listen,' said Max abruptly, 'I was trying to stop all of this from happening, the truck, the explosions. Do you think I was the one that caused all this?'

'Max,' said the detective, 'there was no one else suspicious recorded around the area at the time.'

Max was put back in the cell. More hours passed till at last he heard voices outside the door. It was the sound of his mother and father.

'I hope he's alright,' came the voice of Jenny from the other side of the prison door. Then the prison porthole opened, Max standing up.

Making his way to the porthole he saw his mum and dad standing there on the other side.

'Well the police have told us everything,' said the father, looking concerned. 'Of course we don't believe them, but it'll take time. I'll have to file a lawsuit, I'll have to…' The father stopped what he was saying.

'Oh Max,' said Jenny, 'We believe you're innocent. We've never seen you do anything to harm anyone. This whole thing is ludacris.'

Max hated to see his mother so upset. It was clear for certain that he had been framed.

For now Max would have to make do with his surroundings. Max was monitored 24/7 by security, but Max, who knew he had done nothing wrong, felt a quiet peace in himself as he went about his day within the prison. In his room he read books, played games. There was even a community youth offenders centre he was allowed to visit for two hours each time. There he made friends, quietly going about his business. Of course there was heavy monitoring around him everywhere he went. For after all they did suspect that he was responsible for what had happened at the parade, even if Max knew this wasn't the case at all. Yet Max felt an inner peace as he made friends going too and from his personal cell to the youth offenders centre and back.

Wayne and Jenny sat in front of the television watching the news in the dark of the living room. There on the television sat the newsreader. 'Maximilian Fritz, the teenage suspect linked to the scenes of the Chicago Downtown Parade last week has officially been detained.'

'How could they do something like that, to just a kid,' cried the mum, burying her head on her husband's shoulder.

'Fritz, the only recorded suspect at the scene of the crime,' continued the newsreader, 'was seen to be out amongst the parade, before more events unfolded. A first explosion was set off at exactly 12.36pm that Saturday by a secluded clock tower garden. Moments later another explosion happened, at approximately the same location. What follows next remains to be fully investigated, but the FBI, police and scientists are claiming it was like a 'big show' produced by pyrotechnics, engineering and all other things, scientific. Here is footage showing Max pretending to stop a large truck, 'overturned' from the explosion from hitting the crowds of the parade.'

The newsreader continued, 'Approximately ninety seconds later a third explosion went off at Chicago town hall, whereby just moments before Max was found at the scene, this time caught by a journalist by photograph, with his hands on what appeared to be the explosives just moments before the third large explosion went off. It remains to be said whether there are other people connected to these crimes.'

The father turned off the TV.

'Do you think he'll be alright?' said Jenny, turning to Wayne.

'I'm sure Max will be behaving himself just fine,' said the father. 'Besides, this is just ludacris what they're saying.'

'I just sure hope he's ok,' said the mum.

13

The two men continued working on the project, it nearing completion.

'Hey Boss, check this out,' called one of the men.

The boss stopped what he was doing, drilling in the few remaining screws that kept the rotating engines into place.

The jetpack was looking more finished than ever before, its black metallic shine glowing in the light of the abandoned

94

warehouse, the boss taking a step back from it before reverting his attention to his employee sitting in the corner, by the desk and the TV.

'Seems the boy is still alive,' said the man, watching the news. 'Only half the plan worked, Boss. Look, there he is stepping inside a prison.'

What his employee said was true, the boss watching on as the news footage showed Max being escorted from a car by policemen, the paparazzi surrounding him taking pictures from all angles, Max making his way handcuffed inside the building. For the first few seconds the boss just stood there. Then slowly it was as if a feeling of complete anger engrossed his whole being as he watched the events on the TV play out.

'Well... we'll have to do something about it... Again...' he said finally, gritting his teeth.

'How was he not killed!?' he whispered under his breath.

Turning to his jetpack once more he pointed to some more remaining spots that needed drilling.

The men in the warehouse continued to prepare the boss' jetpack working busy into the night. The boss upon completion looked at it, standing back from it, observing its wings that looked like those of a fighter jet. Then there were the rotating engines that allowed the pilot to fly vertically or horizontally within the split of a second. The boss was happy with the build, yet he knew something still wasn't quite complete…

That same evening the boss drove his car into the warehouse, reversing it slowly in.

The boss shut the door to his car, making his way around to the trunk.

Opening the trunk he revealed two large, metallic shining boxes that looked very important.

'What are these?' said one of his men pointing to one of the boxes, the boss carefully lifting them out.

'These are the '*piece de resistance*," he said, opening the first case with a key. 'What good is a fighter jet without ammunition? What good is a tank without high explosive rounds?' There in the metallic box sat what appeared to a small turret moulded above a rocket projectile.

'It's perfect,' said the boss.

The boss spent the next thirty minutes installing the weapons to his jetpack, the three watching on in wonder. Yet something inside the minds of one of the three employees began to change as he saw the boss drill on the weapons to the flying machine. The man began to think more carefully about what he was being involved in as he watched the boss drill on the final turret to the corner of the wing. *What on earth does the Boss want to use these for?* questioned the man to himself.

Then the man began to think of the events that unfolded at the parade, how they had secretly planted the explosives there, how he had been asked by the boss to disguise himself as a journalist and frame the boy at the townhall. The man began to weigh his actions. *Didn't he realise they had put innocent lives at risk?* He was used to stealing/thieving from others, but to put people in danger in this way, he wasn't sure if he was about that kind of thing. He looked on as he watched his boss look in admiration at the new weapons attached to the pair of wings. It was then that the man decided he would quit the group. Slowly he backed away, leaving the warehouse.

The man hovered in the air as the thrusters of the jetpack burnt, holding the man in perfect balance. The turrets turned and the rocket projectiles swivelled in perfect unison. Slowly the man hovered to the ground as the engines turned off, the widespread wings of his machine pert and polished looking.

'Eureka,' whispered the man to himself as he unstrapped himself from the jetpack, the other two men looking on amazed. 'Gentleman,' he said, 'let us have a toast

97

to our success,' Picking up a glass of champagne he had poured out earlier on a nearby table he handed the men the drinks, wondering where on earth the third team member was. Finishing the champagne glass he looked around, no site of the man anywhere. 'So what do you think?' he said, grinning to the other two men nearby.

'It's amazing, Boss,' said one.

'Fantastic,' said the other.

******

Klara stepped outside onto the porch of her house.

'Mum, I'll just be ten minutes,' she called out, looking down the road towards where the city of Chicago lay in the distance. It was a cool summer's day in August, the sunset red as she took a few clunky steps down the stairs of the patio and out onto the sidewalk. She picked up her DSLR camera hanging around her neck and started looking out in all directions, the calm breeze of the wind making the trees dance with small movements. Breathing a sigh she made her way down the road, looking for any opportunities of a photo, whether it be of the trees or the squirrels or anything that might catch her attention. Klara did have her mind on other things too. Seeing Max on the news like that made her wonder why she ever started liking him in the first place.

She didn't know what to think. *Maybe he was a criminal... maybe he did deserve all this negative media attention, she thought.* She just didn't know.

Closing the door behind her Klara made her way into the living room, her mum watching the news on the TV. The TV flashed showing images of what appeared to be someone stepping outside a prison escorted by guards as the paparazzi took pictures. The newsreader spoke.

'Maximillian Fritz the teenage superhero has been acquitted of all charges following a recent leak from an unknown individual, giving important evidence to the crime scenes at the Downtown Chicago Parade 7 days ago. Police are still unsure of who this man is, though it is likely the man has fled an underground organisation within recent weeks. The leak stated that Maximillian Fritz is in fact innocent and had nothing to do with the crimes. The leak has proven to have taken effect as police have found a secret stash of explosives at coordinates given by the leak - the same explosives used the day at the parade along with fingerprints and more evidence to suggest it was masterminded by someone else entirely.'

'Max!' cried Klara.

******

99

The man slipped out of the back of the warehouse letting his boss and the other colleague finish their work, the sound of drilling in the background. The man drove into the city nervously. Stopping his car, he placed a chip on his phone and rang the police, his number withheld. Using a voice-changer, he gave the location of the boss.

******

'And you're sure he isn't anywhere to be found?' said the boss, angrily. 'Well isn't this just great?' he exclaimed.

Then it occurred to the boss that he might have known exactly what was going on, as he went back to polishing his new jetpack. Moments later the boss threw his polishing cloth to the ground, a look of anger on his face as he began to go about readying his things.

'I should have known,' he said as he ran over to the desk, collecting papers of blueprints and other important stuff. Stuffing them into a leather briefcase he slung it over his shoulder. 'We've got to go, and fast,' he said, calling out to the other two men.

'What do you mean?' said one, looking on curiously. 'We've only just finished the jetpack. Why rush off so soon?'

'I haven't got any time to explain,' said the boss as he began wheeling out the jetpack situated on a mobile platform. 'Drive to West Virginia. Go now and don't stop,' he said. 'Call me when you get there!'

The two men did as they were told. Starting up the car they sped off into the distance.

The boss wasted no time in strapping himself to the jetpack, once outside.

The sound of police cars rang in the distance gradually growing louder, the boss turning on the ignition as he went rocketing up into the air. Like a missile he launched upwards increasing altitude every second, then he changed the angle of the engines heading straight towards the direction of West Virginia.

The policeman slammed the break, his car skidding to a stop outside the abandoned warehouse. Getting out of his car he looked up as the flying object flew further and further into the sky.

******

The deputy chief policeman twiddled his thumbs sitting at the dining room table of the Fritz household that afternoon.

'Here's your water, sir,' said Jenny, giving the cold glass of water to the deputy. Jenny took a seat. Max and his father were already at the table.

'So you're saying that my son has… superpowers…?' said Jenny.

'That's right,' nodded the policeman.

'And where did they come from exactly?' said the father.

'We're still yet to find out, but it's clear that what Max possesses is 'other-worldly.' A great strength, many times of a man's that's for sure, as well as his ability to *jump*.'

There was silence.

'Mr and Mrs. Fritz, may we use your garden for a second?' said the deputy, looking at Max.

'Now Max, why don't you show your parents how you can *jump*,' said the deputy, the four standing out in the Fritz's garden, the sun shining.

Max, without wasting any time threw himself high into the air, the parents watching on as he flew vertically higher than that of around two multi storey buses. Max landed back on the grass with ease.

The face of the parents turned white.

'And now why not horizontally,' said the deputy.

Max propelled himself into the air, jumping at least two horizontal buses in distance. The parent's faces continued to look white.

Back at the dining room table there was an even longer silence, the parents sitting there in complete bewilderment. 'And why didn't you tell us?' said Mr. Fritz, at long last, looking at Max.

'I didn't want to cause any attention,' said Max, solemnly.

'That's not all,' said the deputy. He pulled out a tablet from his bag, switching it on he slid it across the table for the parents to see. There on the tablet showed CCTV footage of Max fighting the man outside the bakery, and then of the crime scene with the lady's bag and then footage of the stolen car.

'Oh my!' said Jenny. There was an even longer pause.

'As you can see Max has been combining his Taekwondo skills with his strength and his ability to jump. He has been offering the city a service at nighttime. Not every night mind you. In fact it was only three times you went out and helped against Chicago crime. Wasn't that right Max?'

'Yes,' said Max.

'So…' said Mr. Fritz after another long silence, the mother and father in disbelief. 'I guess it wouldn't harm to

103

ask who exactly caused the attacks on the parade then? After all that's been said and done.'

'His name is David Cohen,' said the deputy. 'He is an ex-pilot for the air force as well as an engineer. He is responsible for what happened at the parade.'

The deputy took the last sip of his drink as he looked at the time. 'Alright, I'm afraid I must go—' he said.

Mr. Fritz stood up immediately and walked the deputy to the door.

'It's been a pleasure meeting you Mr. Fritz,' said the deputy.

Mr. Fritz said nothing.

'If you have any more questions, do let me know,' said the deputy, and with that he left.

It took a while for the Fritz household to get used to the fact of Max's superhero ability. But now the whole world knew who Max was too, the media lining the streets of Max's house for any chance to see the teenage superhero. The mother and father were not really pleased at the constant traffic down their road with journalists and everybody else that wanted Max for a photograph. But quickly they realised they would have to make do and get used to the fact that the natural fascination for Max's ability would probably never die down.

'Just be safe when you're out,' called the mother to Max as he opened the front door to go out.

'Hey Max,' said one of the paparazzi on the sidewalk in front of their garden, taking a photo, the rest of the paparazzi taking photos, as Max made his way to the nearest bus stop.

That afternoon Max planned to meet Klara for a drink at Juice Bar in town. Max knew the paparazzi would be there, and surely enough there they were lined up at the windows taking photographs while the two sipped on their drinks. Max thought of all the possible headlines that might be in the newspapers the following day, 'Max's new love affair,' or 'Max's latest lover seen out in town with Max.' In some ways Max found it quite funny how the paparazzi were so interested in him, but ultimately he knew he had to get on with his own life and enjoy every second of it. Max enjoyed his time with Klara at the juice bar and before they left he even leant in for a kiss which Klara reciprocated. Today was a good day and eventually it was time for Max to go home.

'So Max, can I assume it was you who saved me at the pier?' Klara said smiling, shutting the door to Juice Bar behind her.

'Yes,' said Max, smiling back. 'Yes, it was me.'

It had been exactly two weeks since Max had been released from prison and to be honest Max felt good. In no way did he particularly feel damaged or bitter, he just felt happy to be out, knowing in himself he had done nothing wrong.

That night the phone rang at the Fritz household.

'Fritz home,' said the mum.

'Mrs. Fritz… we need to talk.' It was the deputy.

'Wayne, that's completely out of the question,' cried Jenny in disbelief. 'Your home is here, in Chicago, it's where we've always been.'

'Well…' said the father, 'They said they needed Max's help. It looks like David Cohen can't be stopped. They've already spotted him twice in New York City. They said he was even seen travelling from West Virginia to New York the other day. Think of the disaster that man could reap.'

Max sat quietly in the car. Looking solemn he listened to some music, one of his earbuds dropping out, placing it back in his ear. Max's father sat quiet in the front. Max didn't like to see his mother upset, yet it seemed like this time it couldn't be helped. All of Max's things were in the trunk of the car as Max's father drove to New York City that night.

The morning came and the Fritz car came to a halt, the bustling city of New York around them. Max's father grinned. 'Well I thought I'd keep it a surprise Max, but looks like this is where we're gonna be staying for the unseeable future.'

Max looked up at the site of a hotel through the car window, a vast skyscraper that stood planted in the sky.

'Says who?' cried Max, in excitement.

'Says the deputy,' said the father, turning in his seat, looking at Max in disbelief sitting in the back of the car.

'Alright then,' said Max, keeping his cool, not wanting to show his father too much excitement. Max got out of the car, his father walking to the back, opening the trunk. Before he could grab Max's suitcase he was interrupted by someone standing close by.

'Not to worry sir, I'll take that,' said the hotel porter springing into action, looking smart in his full attire.

Max's eyes widened, looking up at the hotel skyscraper with its never-ending floors scaling high into the sky. The glossy clean look of the windows shone in the New York sun. Max took a few short breaths as he made his way up the flight of stairs that led to the entrance of the hotel. Quietly the porter behind them wheeled the suitcase over to where the entrance was. Inside the reception, vast, squeaky clean marble floors stretched out in all directions with an expensive red rug covering the floor by the leather reception couches and chairs.

'Maximillian Fritz to check in,' said Mr. Fritz, standing by his son at the reception desk. Max took in his surroundings seeing other people go by, different customers and hotel workers passing through the reception, the lift ringing as the guests went into the elevators, disappearing out of sight.

'Well Gentlemen,' said the receptionist, 'it looks like the Penthouse Suite is all yours. Here's your keys.'

The receptionist handed the pair of keys to Max's father.

'Put it in your pocket Max,' said Mr. Fritz handing Max one of them, 'and make sure you don't lose them.'

The lift quietly embarked on its journey, passing all the floors reaching the top of the hotel. Slowly the doors opened leading to a short corridor that gave way to three or four more rooms, including the Penthouse Suite.

The suite was nothing like Max had ever seen. Big enough to fit four normal sized rooms all in one space with its high ceiling, a king size bed and a whopper sized TV on the wall, it made Max feel like he was all set.

'There's some beverages here,' said the hotel assistant pointing to a silver table in the middle of the room. 'There's

Fanta, Cola and if there's anything else you'd like to eat or drink you can always contact me by telephone. The phone's right by your bed if you need anything,' said the porter. At that the porter left the room.

'Wow,' said Max, 'I've never seen a place like this before, you mean this is all for us?'

'I guess so,' said Mr. Fritz. 'For now anyway.'

Max stepped out onto the penthouse suite balcony. He looked out at the city, the other skyscrapers in the distance, some even taller than the one he was on now. He could hear the sounds of cars below, the smog and the light of the sky intertwining into the distance. He looked out and saw the Statue of Liberty, the Empire state building, and all the other buildings that were placed within the heart of the city.

The next few days Max did nothing in particular. There was no phone call from the deputy, no alarms raised whatsoever. Instead Max played video games, enjoyed the swimming pool at the very top of the hotel above his suite. All the things that you'd want to do in a hotel Max did. Occasionally Max went outside, but being swamped by the paparazzi on the high street Max preferred to stay inside the hotel. Soon Max got to know some of the names that worked there. Joanne who did the laundry, then there was Diego at the reception and Serenity, the catering manager at the hotel restaurant.

Max was at the side of the swimming pool when his phone rang.

'Hey Max, it's me Chuck,' came the voice of Chuck on the other line. 'How's everything going in New York?'

'Well….' said Max.

'I'm gonna cut to the chase Max, I'm coming down to NYC to visit you! I'm on the road now!'

'Really!' cried Max on the phone, 'no way!'

'This is a great place you got here,' said Chuck climbing out of his mum's car, the pair making their way inside.

After playing on the games console on the massive TV in Max's suite for a couple hours, soon enough the two wondered what they should do next. 'You wanna go shopping?' said Chuck, after a few moments of thinking.

'Sure,' said Max.

The clicks of the paparazzi flashed as the photographers took their pictures, from the other side of the entrance to the hotel.

'I mean, is it safe to go out?' said Chuck as the pair stood by the entrance, seeing the many paparazzi on the other side of the doors.

'Ah what the heck,' said Max finally, storming his way out, Chuck following behind.

'Max! Over here Max! Max, over here!' came the voices of the different paparazzi from all around.

Inside the city Max and Chuck had the biggest blast imaginable. With the money Max's father had given him for his time in New York, Max and Chuck used it on the arcade, for restaurants, for every cool thing in New York. There was the cinema, then the basketball jerseys. In fact at one point Max wondered if they would ever stop spending.

In the afternoon Max and Chuck went to a cool burger restaurant on 32nd street with the view of the Empire State Building just down the road. There they ate a gigantic burger each, with melting cheese and bacon, one of the menu specials. The sun started to set in the sky, both Max and Chuck feeling relaxed as the pair ate the last of their meal. Max was satisfied with his purchases from the little shopping spree he and Chuck had had. There was the New York Knicks jersey he had brought from the sports store as well as a video game and a book.

The day was beginning to end, the sunset more orangy than ever. Max couldn't stop looking outside the window at the table he and Chuck were at, thinking about his day in the city, and even about Klara.

*****

David Cohen read the headlines of the newspaper he picked up, walking out of the metro in amidst the bustling city of New York. He was wearing sunglasses and a hoodie over his head.

'So the boy's in town,' he chuckled to himself, tossing the paper in the trash.

'Perfect,' he said.

14

Klara made her way out into the garden of her home that evening just as the sun was about to set. She wanted to take some last-minute photos before it got dark. In the distance lay the river that ran right outside her house, down the hill of the garden. There she could see the water's reflection, the sun dimming in the sky leaving all its colours. She took pictures of the water, then back to the flowers on the sides of the lawn. When she had gotten as many photos as she needed she stopped and looked out once more to the river, sighing. *How was Max doing in New York?* she wondered. She had seen him on the TV in the news.

******

Max tossed and turned in bed. Strangely with all the fun times Max had had in New York recently, Max still felt a small sense of worry. That night he couldn't stop thinking about David. *What if he was to show himself in New York? What if he were to attack again?*

The thought of it stayed in the back of his mind as he tried to get some sleep.

The next morning Max woke up with a slight headache. He sat up in bed looking around him, the television set still on. His dad had gone out for the morning it seemed, Chuck still sleeping on the mattress on the floor.

Then he walked to the poolside above, the bright morning sunshine filling the sky, the pool outside all serene looking.

Max walked downstairs again and got himself some orange juice from the fridge, then made himself a slice of toast.

Chuck still asleep, Max sidestepped around his mattress, Chuck still making the snoring noises he would normally make all night.

It was an unusually fresh morning, the sun firmly in the sky, Max taking a bite to eat from his toast. Out on the balcony he looked across the city to Liberty Island, the Statue of Liberty in the New York harbour, the glistening water in the distance.

It was as if it came out of nowhere when it happened, a huge explosion sound, the faint sound of screams as the earth shuddered. There, in the distance, was a great explosion next to the Financial District, located at Battery Park where across the harbour the Statue of Liberty was situated.

Max knew it was David Cohen. Without any second to spare Max took the elevator down to reception, adrenaline in him flowing. Just as he had reached the bottom floor his phone began to ring. It was the deputy.

'Max,' said the deputy on the other line, 'David…'

'I know,' said Max, 'don't worry, I've got this.'

And with that Max hung up the phone, running outside the hotel entrance, pushing past all the paparazzi, who looked confused upon hearing the explosion too.

Traffic continued as normal.

Max ran down the long avenues in the direction of Battery Park, in front of the harbour.

Running along the street Max soared into the air, jumping his way down the street, dodging all the people on the sidewalk until he finally landed on a double decker that took him en route to Battery Park.

Jumping off the roof of the double decker bus, he looked up hearing the familiar sound of David's jetpack, this time even more powerful sounding than before, watching him spiral into the sky leaving a chemtrail.

Amidst Battery Park, Max watched as David Cohen spiralled upwards, stopping, then spiralling down the way he came.

As David came soaring down it was clear that David had spotted Max, David falling from the sky, faster and faster, gliding straight towards him.

Max started to run, David swooping down on him, beginning to fire the two turrets strapped to either wing. Luckily Max being able to run fast sped down the park paths, the bullets from the turrets tearing up the concrete pathways, Max narrowly dodging the gunfire.

David Cohen swooped back into the air regaining his height, people running and screaming in all directions, to avoid any sort of repeat.

Cohen never kept his eyes off Max as Max ran into the Financial District, weaving in and out of panicked passers-by. Cohen stalled in the air, watching with eagle eyes, Max running in and out of the busy city-goers of New York.

Max turned around and saw Cohen coming ever closer. Unsure of how to bring down the flying man he watched on helplessly.

As like before, David Cohen swooped down over Max, picking him up like a bird of prey. Together they flew through the air.

Thinking he could finish Max once and for all David let go of Max sending him crashing through the windows of the nearest financial office skyscraper, David swooping sideways narrowly missing the skyscraper himself.

Max, still alive, stood up from all the glass that had entered the office building, people behind their desks watching in horror as Max came crashing through the window.

David Cohen circled around the skyscraper, like a man toying with his food, seeing if Max was still alive or not through the large glass windows of the building.

Max, daring to do the ultimate thing, got back up to his feet and jumped back out of the smashed window, just in time, crash landing on top of David Cohen's jetpack as he came round the corner, Max holding on for dear life. Max gripped tight onto the back of the jetpack, David sensing Max was on top of him soared through the air the opposite way of the harbour, towards the hotel in which Max was staying in. David climbed higher and higher into the air, Max holding on for dear life. Seeing that Max wouldn't budge, not even by the speed of the jetpack, David tried the opposite thing and spiralled downwards, towards the top of the hotel in which Max was staying, the pool on the rooftop directly in site. They rocketed down towards the top of the hotel, the rest of the city in view. Max realising that no one was going to win at this rate, did the unimaginable. With all his might he pushed himself down on the back of the jetpack sending it into a course collision with the rooftop of the hotel. Absolutely obliterating the top of the rooftop, Max jumped off just in time rolling onto the decking beside the swimming pool crashing landing into the barbeque set and everything else that was there. The impact of the collision of the jetpack was so strong that there was a mighty crash as it tore through the upper decking of the swimming pool, crashing down through the decking and through the ceiling of Max's penthouse suite.

Chuck, who was frying some scrambled eggs in the kitchen of the penthouse, was listening to music on his earphones and thought he had heard something. Turning around he took off his headphones and looked back through the bedroom seeing the horrific sight before him.

Max woke from consciousness, his vision blurry at first. He had lost his glasses, but it didn't matter now. Quickly he stood up, seeing the damage, the whole rooftop collapsed in, the pool water flooding into the penthouse suite below.

'Max?' came a voice from the suite, the chlorine water rushing in at a rapid pace, the roof almost fully collapsed.

'Chuck is that you?' cried Max scurrying down the broken roof into the suite, water everywhere.

'Max!' came the voice of Chuck.

Max clambered down and looked around him, until his eyes finally met Chuck who was standing by the kitchen where the roof had not collapsed in.

'I was just frying some eggs!?' said Chuck, standing there with a spatula and a very shocked face.

'Max, did you see a man climb out of the wreckage?' said Max, over to Chuck.

'No, I just heard the noise over my headphones, then this!'

Eventually Max began to feel a sudden surge of pain in his right arm.

Soon enough the alarms went off all around the hotel, everyone evacuating the building by the stairs. Outside the entrance people crowded around, wondering what on earth had just happened. Police cars began driving to the scene as well as fire engines and anyone else that might be there to help.

Max and Chuck mingled their way through the crowds.

'Max!' came the voice of Max's father, rushing through the people. Max turned around. There was his father squeezing through the crowds coming towards him.

'Oh Max, I'm so glad you're safe,' he said, stopping at Max's feet. 'What happened out there? Was it David?'

'Yes,' said Max, 'yes, it was David.'

'Dad,' said Max, 'I think I've hurt my arm, I think we need to get it checked.'

'We will,' said Max's father, finally. 'From now you're staying with me boys,' said Mr. Fritz, beckoning them to follow him to his car.

Just at that moment there was a call in the distance amongst the crowds.

'Mr. Fritz!' came the voice of the deputy, mingling through the people. Seconds later the deputy was by Mr. Fritz, the pair speaking, Max looking on.

'Thank you Mr. Deputy,' said Wayne at long last, 'but from now I want to look after my own kids, thank you very much.'

There was a concerned look on the deputy's face. 'I understand,' he said.

15

'Where does it hurt exactly?' said the father, Chuck and Max sitting in the backseat of Mr. Fritz' car, Mr. Fritz driving through the streets of New York.

'I'm not sure exactly, just the lower part of my arm,' said Max.

'Alright,' said Wayne, 'We'll get you to a hospital, but first let's first make sure we're well out of the city before anything else bad happens here. Can you hold it for much longer Max?' said the father.

'I'll be fine,' said Max.

Slowly Max's father made their way out of the city, Max sensing a slight panic about the city-goers on the streets, the news already spread about the explosion at Battery Park as well as the strange flying jetpack in the sky.

'Max,' I think I'm being followed,' said Mr. Fritz once they were out of the city, about forty or so minutes of driving since their journey began. Max looked through the back window of the car. Surely enough there was a black SUV car trailing behind them.

Then it started to rain, the skies becoming darker, Mr. Fritz's window wipers beginning to go from side to side.

'That car has been following me ever since the city,' said Max's father, the rain falling harder.

'What are we going to do?' said Max, sensing the danger in his father's voice. Chuck kept silent.

'Well we can't stop now, it's pouring outside. We'll have to continue moving. If they haven't disappeared in twenty minutes, well...'

'They might be David's men,' said Max.

******

Klara was painting in the dining room of her house in the suburbs of Chicago, the sunset red. Carefully she drew the three oranges and apple that lay still on the dining room table before her. Her mum, watching the TV in the living room, flicked channels until she got to the news.

121

'There has been recorded an explosion in Battery Park this morning, in New York City, by the city's great harbour at approximately 10.30am,' said the newsreader.

'Wait,' cried Klara from the dining room, 'Don't change channels … Max!' cried Klara, watching the television set, the explosion caught on footage from around the city.

'Oh my!' said Klara's mother.

'Max is in New York right now,' exclaimed Klara. 'Mum, I'm gonna call him!' she cried.

Max's phone rang. The rain was still pouring down as Max's father drove down the street on the way to Delaware.

'Max, are you alright!?' said Klara.

'Everything's ok,' said Max. 'We're out of the city now. Everything's fine. But Klara, we're kinda busy. I'll call you later, ok?' And with that Max hung up the phone.

Klara wasn't sure if everything was really alright, but trusting Max nonetheless she let it go. Klara continued to watch the rest of the news report.

The rain dying down, Max looked around to see if their pursuers were still there.

'Dad,' said Max, 'they're still following us.'

'Right that's it, I'm stopping the car,' said Mr. Fritz suddenly. 'This can't go on any longer,' he said, anger and frustration in his voice.

'But what if they're David's men?' said Max again.

Max's father took some time to think. *What if Max was right? Who knows what could happen if they stopped the car?*

'Forget this!' said Max's father all of a sudden. 'Let's try and lose them.'

And with that he put his foot on the gas, the car lurching forward at a fast pace.

'Dad, they're still not letting up,' said Max, turning around, all the while Chuck remaining silent. The speed of the car grew faster, seventy mph, eighty, ninety... the trees of Delaware forest became ever denser and thicker.

Eventually their car came across another car in front driving along at a slower pace. Mr. Fritz knew that he would have to overtake the car to lose those pursuing, yet being on a bend in the road meant their view was blocked ahead — forcing them to slow down and be caught, or to lurch on ahead. Mr. Fritz, taking the chance, passed the car in front, yet due to bad timing drove the car off the road due to another oncoming car. The wheels screeched as Wayne slammed on the brakes, the car speeding along the side of the tarmac, and into a tree. There the forest was directly in front of them, the car forced to a complete halt.

123

Luckily no one was harmed, yet smoke from the front bumper of the car started to spread out into the air.

'Quick, get out!' cried Mr. Fritz.

The three opened their doors and immediately ran into the forest as the car behind them came to a screeching halt.

Weaving in and out of the trees the three ran and ran, running for their lives. Behind them were three men.

'Dad, they've got guns!' cried Max turning his head as the first of the men pulled out a firearm from his pocket, pulling the trigger.

A mighty 'CRACK—' sounded behind them. Max felt the zip of a bullet pass as they shuffled and wove through the trees. They ran and ran, the three running hotly behind.

'Quick over here,' said Mr. Fritz suddenly, leering to the left where before them was a large steep hill. Mr. Fritz slid over the ledge of the hill. Getting up to his feet, he scrambled under a ledge that seemed to overlook the hill.

'Over here,' he whispered as the two boys climbed down and followed him. 'Stay quiet,' whispered Mr. Fritz as they huddled together, keeping as coldly still as possible under the ledge. They listened to the sounds of shouts and the tread of feet from above.

'I could have sworn I saw them go this way?' said one voice, the three keeping as deadly silent as possible.

'...Wait until Boss hears about this,' said another.

'They gotta be around here somewhere. Come on!' said a third, and with that Max heard the sound of the three men scurry off, the dust of the forest floor kicking up in their tracks.

The three boys continued running through Delaware Forest. Not taking any chances they ran and ran.

'Guys, wait up,' called Chuck eventually as he stopped, bending over, out of breath. Mr. Fritz stopped, turning around scanning the forest for any signs of the three men.

'It's alright Chuck,' he said finally. 'We'll walk...'

The two boys followed Mr. Fritz through the woods, Chuck still panting and breathing heavily.

It was the afternoon now and the sun was strangely high in the sky as Max wiped the sweat from his brow. A few minutes later there appeared to be a clearing in the woods, the trees hiding what appeared to be an open field with a lake and an old wooden house situated by it, with an old banged up looking truck beside it.

'Look there's a house over there,' pointed Max to the old looking cabin.

'I'm tired. I need a drink,' said Chuck as he bent over again, the running getting to him.

'Listen, we'll go to the house,' said the father, 'maybe get some water there or something. But keep an eye out,' he said.

The father knocked on the door of the cabin, quietly at first then louder.

'Alright, I'm coming,' eventually came the quiet voice of a woman. 'You woke me from my nap,' she said softly as she opened the door.

'Who are you?' she said finally, the light from outside blinding her for a few short moments, before raising a hand to shade her gaze.

'My name's Mr. Fritz,' said Wayne.

She paused, eyeing down the three men from top to bottom. 'Alright,' she said, 'Well do come in.'

'You want some soda?' she said moving over to the kitchen, in the one roomed cabin with kitchen, bedroom and the little restroom suite all included in the one space.

'Sure,' said Max. Chuck remained silent.

'So…' she said softly, 'what's the likes of you doing in the middle of Delaware Forest?' she said.

'Oh… we're… um…. just here for a vacation,' said Mr. Fritz. 'We thought we'd visit the forest today and we got lost so…'

'The forest can do that to you sometimes' she said, kindly, interrupting. 'Yes, sometimes it has a way of always looking the same.'

'Your accent?' said Wayne, interjecting, 'but if I'm correct, it's…'

'Not from around here?' she said. 'Oh I know… What's a girl like me, doing up in Delaware more like?' she chuckled. 'Well to tell you the truth my husband lived here once, God rest his soul. It wasn't that long ago he died, mind you, say two years ago. I guess my heart belongs here now, in this forest. I come from Tennessee you see, and at first when my husband left me I wanted to go back home. But something in me said, 'give this place a chance. If my husband liked it, then so will I," she said. 'There's something in the air up here that springs magic, you know… you know what I mean?'

'Yes… I think I can understand,' said Mr. Fritz.

The three boys listened contently to the young woman, Max's arm still in pain, but listening anyway. She talked about her new life in Delaware, the woman talking as if she had never really spoken to anyone for a long time. The three of them were captivated by her until at last Mr. Fritz, realising the time, looked at his watch.

'Oh my, the time has flown,' he said.

127

'You mean I've been talking all this time and none of you have said a word,' she said, interjecting. 'Bless your souls,' she said, softly. 'Tell me,' she said, 'before you leave, what are your boy's names?'

'Well,' said Wayne, tired, wondering if the woman would ever believe them anyway. 'I don't know if you have watched the news recently, but this is… Maximillian Fritz… the teenage superhero… I guess you could say… well he's been on the news and everything as of late,' said Mr. Fritz, truthfully.

'I'm sorry, I don't watch the TV that much,' she said. 'I prefer a good novel. But having said that the name does kinda ring a bell. Say it again one more time.'

'Maximillian Fritz?' said Mr. Fritz.

'…Yes, I think I've heard it been said. Can't remember from where exactly though, maybe it was my friend Sandra who said it? But, superhero you say? Now what exactly is that supposed to mean?'

'Well… Max, he has abilities, like he possesses a great strength, and the ability to jump long distances, and he can fight.'

'Fight?' she said, 'Well I've heard of young men being able to do that, but jump, you say? How far?' she said, finally.

'Tell her,' said Mr. Fritz, looking at Max.

'Oh about 70 metres on a good day,' said Max.

The young woman looked at them blankly, as if they had just gone mad. '70 metres!?' she said, 'Have you guys gone crazy?' she said.

'Well…' said Mr. Fritz interjecting. 'In actual fact we're on the run from a criminal organisation that wants to try and kill Max. Sees Max as a threat or something.'

The lady looked at them like they really had gone completely mad. Just then there was a knock at the door.

'That could be them-' whispered Mr. Fritz. Mr. Fritz scurried to the corner of the cabin, beckoning the two boys to hide with him.

'What on earth?' thought the woman as she stood up to get the door.

There at the door stood three men out of breath each of them wearing black t-shirts and jeans. The young woman was quick to spot firearms strapped to their pockets. 'Oh…' she whispered, looking up, seeing them look sweaty and out of breath.

'You don't happen to have seen a man and two boys around here have you?' said one of the men.

The woman gave herself some time to think, realising that maybe her guests might have been right all along.

'Oh… well… I can't say that I have,' she said as she covered the door. In a split second she beckoned to the three hiding to go out the back, shielding an arm behind her — signalling to the back door. The three in the corner did as they were told, not making a sound.

'You sure about that young lady?' said one of the men.

'Oh I'm sure,' she said as she stepped to the side letting the men peer into the one roomed cabin, once she was sure the other three had properly hid. After a few moments of looking around from the doorway, the three men went on their way.

'And you say they're after you?' said the woman finally when the men had gone.

'Yes,' said Max. 'We think they're David Cohen's men. David Cohen, a great fighter jet engineer… who used to work for the American Air Force.'

'Right…' said the lady, another confused look on her face.

'Well,' she said, 'you boys sure do live adventurous lives.'

'Well that was an interesting afternoon,' said the woman as Mr. Fritz and the boys got themselves ready to go, taking a few more sips of their soda.

'Now listen,' she said, as they were about to leave. 'I think I can be a help to you. The nearest train station is

130

about a thirty-minute drive from here. I suppose y'all can hitchhike a lift with me to the station if one of you doesn't mind sitting in the back.'

'Well to tell you the truth,' said Mr. Fritz, 'Max really needs a doctor. Don't you Max?' he said.

The mini truck jostled and bounced as it made its way through Delaware Forest on the way to the nearest hospital. The whole time the two boys kept under the window of the truck, Mr. Fritz in the back laying down so as not to be seen by the three of Cohen's men.

******

Klara kept her eyes fixed on the apple trying with every ounce of her being to draw the outer lines of the fruit the way she saw it. Carefully she started to add in 'shade,' giving the fruit texture and shape. Suddenly the phone rang.

'What now?' she whispered, making her way to the phone. It was Max.

'Klara!' said Max on the other end.

'Hey Max,' said Klara.

'Klara I'm so sorry about earlier,' said Max.

'It's ok Max,' said Klara. 'The explosion on the news,' she said slowly, 'in New York, where were you when it happened?' she asked.

'Listen, I'll tell you later, I'm on the train back to Chicago, Chucks here and so is my father. We're all safe, I promise. But we'll talk about it soon, ok?'

16

That weekend Chuck and Max could be found at the arcade, playing 'Zombies of the Apocalypse,' their favourite game, shooting down the grotesque figures that marched and trudged their way towards them. It turned out that Max's injury was just a light sprain, and that the pain would quickly go away. Chuck, subdued by recent events, quickly found his rhythm again once the game had started. 'Quick get the one in the corner,' he shouted as they shot and defamed the flying zombie bat that swooped in and attacked them from the left-hand side of the screen.

Soon enough it was time for them to leave the arcade.

'So people call you the teenage superhero huh?' he said, inquiring, the pair walking down the road to the bus-stop.

'Yes, I guess so,' said Max.

132

'Have you tried flying?' said Chuck, curiously. 'Do you also have laser vision?'

'No,' said Max laughing, 'I have neither.'

There was laughter and cheeriness all around as the Fritz family, Chuck and Klara dined out in the city of Chicago.

Eventually the waiter came over to take their bill.

Jenny sighed. 'I just don't wanna think about what happened to you in New York,' she chuckled, gazing out of the window of the restaurant.

'There there,' said Mr. Fritz, 'It wasn't all that bad was it Max?' said Mr. Fritz winking to Max.

'No of course not,' said Max, smiling.

'Good,' said Mrs. Fritz. 'Our lives have gone mad ever since you've acquired your abilities, wouldn't you say Max?' she said.

Mr Fritz quickly cut in. 'Now I know things have been stressful recently… Which is why I've decided we're all due a holiday… and where better to go… than the sunny state of California! You're both invited, Chuck and Klara! I'll pay for it. We'll have a blast. What do you guys say?'

'Sure,' said Chuck and Klara, excitedly.

'There's so many things to see in California, isn't there Max?' said Mr. Fritz. 'There's beaches, amusement parks, the wild outdoors.'

133

Soon enough it was time for the Fritz family and Chuck and Klara to leave the restaurant, the orange sun setting in the sky.

******

The sound of running water was all around as the man came to consciousness, like someone had left the tap on in the room and the water was still running.

David Cohen could feel debris around him… and then there was the feel of the water. He felt the wetness in his hands, his feet and in his pants and shirt.

'Max!' came the sound of a teenage voice outside the rubble. David kept deadly still, there barely enough room within the rubble to breath. And the water… it came from the pool… *the roof must have collapsed in when they hit the rooftop,* thought David. *Speaking of Max, where is he?* he wondered, remaining deadly still.

David laid there in the rubble as he listened out for Max's voice. Eventually it came.

'Max, did you see a man climb out of the wreckage?' came the voice of Max from above, the sound of trickling water everywhere.

'No I just heard a noise over my headphones and then this,' came the first voice.

'My arm,' came the voice of Max, then the sound of someone walking over the pile of wreckage that lay above Cohen. Keeping as still as he could he heard the sound of rummaging and shuffling over the brick and wood on top of him.

Soon enough the sound of the two boys disappeared. Using all his strength David Cohen began to move his body in a way that alleviated himself from the wreckage, pushing his way upwards till at last he could sense he was not far from the top of the debris. Squeezing himself through the roof he created an opening with his hands, throwing bits of wood and brick away from where he was coming out. Squeezing out of the rubble he staggered… then stood up, breathing heavily for more air. Then made his way out the room.

Keeping his head down Cohen made his way down the long flight of stairs of the hotel, different people from the floors and rooms of the hotel joining in on the long journey to the ground floor where the evacuation was happening. Out into the reception David Cohen trudged, through the sliding doors and into the crowd of guests who were waiting out in front. Keeping his head down he squeezed through the numerous people, briefly spotting Max and Chuck in the corner of his eye, never daring to fully look at them in case he was spotted. There he walked through the crowds and out onto the streets of New York City.

As he made his way through the roads he saw panic and fear on many of the faces of the city-goers, policemen and the fire brigade driving up to the hotel. He knew he had accomplished something, causing panic and fear in the city, but as for the boy, well he was still alive, and that would not do. The man continued to walk down the streets of New York until he came to 46th street where the New York Aviation Museum was. Entering through the spinning doors he slipped his way through the line at the ticket desk and made his way into the museum.

Making his way to the back of the building he made his way into one of the exhibits in which he knew well. There positioned in the corner of the room was a huge, model, fighter jet plane and beside it a model jetpack, a replica of the very first working jetpack in history. He fixed his eyes on the jetpack's engines, taking in their concrete and sturdy design, looking at all its mechanical details.

Just then an announcement over the speakerphones rang out from within the room. 'Attention please, would all guests make their way to the entrance. This is an emergency. Would all guests inside the museum make their way to the entrance.'

Mr. Cohen smiled.

Great, he thought. *Panic has spread.*

17

The Fritz SUV slowly set off from the drive of Max's home, Klara sitting securely in the back. It was planned that they would stop by Chuck's on the way to pick him up.

'Oh I'm afraid Chuck has come down with the flu,' said Chuck's mother as Mrs. Fritz slid down the window to speak to Chuck's mother.

'Oh no,' cried Mrs. Fritz, the pair of them falling into conversation quickly. Soon enough after the mums had had their 'mum conversation' it was time for the Fritz family and Klara to go. Down the freeway they drove, all the way from Chicago stopping the one night at a motel, advancing west to California, through Utah, Las Vegas and then on to California. They drove through the desert, through the long roads of the wilderness and out into the countryside, through the casino city, until at last the sunny coasts of California came into view. Klara smiled to herself, Mr. Fritz driving past the same spot Max had saved Klara at St. Monica Pier. The family turned north heading for Yosemite National Park north of Los Angeles.

The family and Klara camped out on the hills of Yosemite Park within the designated areas, the four taking in the fresh air and the natural beauty of the sequoia trees and the rock faces of the cliffs. There they had the perfect view of a waterfall and next to them a river that flowed through the campsite, at one point Mrs. Fritz even hopping in and having a swim.

Later on in the week the Fritz family and Klara were also found jumping off the smaller side cliffs of the waterfall and into the water for a whole afternoon, the four having the most amazing of times. In the evenings they roasted marshmallows by the fire and thought up scary stories to see if they could frighten each other.

'Let me tell you about the strange case of Dr. Jekyll and Mr. Hyde,' said Mr. Fritz as he recited the story to the three listening eagerly by the campfire.

'That's not made-up—' said Mrs. Fritz, laughing.

'I know,' said Mr. Fritz, '...I'm afraid my bucket of horror stories is running kinda dry,' he laughed.

The four waited for the next story to come.

'I've got something,' said Klara, 'Well it's not really a horror-story mind you, and I'm afraid I haven't made it up either. It was one of the stories my mum used to tell me before I went to bed, when I was younger.'

138

The three of the Fritz family kept quiet as Klara began to recite her story.

'It's a Native American story' she added.

'There once were two salmon fish, friends of the same shoal that swam and socialised with one another for days upon days. Through freshwater and seawater they travelled, diving and swimming through rivers, out into the depths of the sea and back to freshwater alike. They loved to dive and swim and even jump out into the air and back into the water again, which could help them reach higher levels inland. One of them had a particular love for jumping out of the water as high as he could go, to show-off to friends and say, 'Look who can jump the highest, me!' The other salmon were jealous of him. His life-long friend saw the darker side of his friend's ability. He warned him not to jump so high so often, particularly inland, because there was the bear who might catch him for a meal. The first salmon didn't listen and continued to jump out from the waters as high as he could go, in and out every day, higher than any other fish. The other fish looked on jealously. Except the day came when the salmon's friend's advice turned out to be right… before it was too late.'

'Oh how sad!' said Mrs. Fritz.

Klara shrugged.

'And what's it supposed to tell us?' said Mr. Fritz.

The three listened as Klara spoke. 'I guess… I guess it tells us that we shouldn't always live to show off, to always seek attention, because sometimes it can get the better of us. Instead we should keep our head down and work and live a good life, I guess… I dunno,' she said. 'That's what my mother told me anyway.'

'Well I liked it,' said Mrs. Fritz, smiling.

'Me too,' said Max.

The time came when Klara and the Fritz family were to pack their things and say goodbye to Yosemite National Park. 'I'm gonna miss this place,' said Mrs. Fritz as she put the last tent into the back of the car.

'I'm gonna miss the roasted marshmallows,' said Mr. Fritz, slinging the camp chair and the stove into the trunk.

'I'm gonna miss the sequoia trees,' said Klara.

'And I'm gonna miss the waterfall,' said Max.

The SUV winded through the small roads of the national park and out onto the freeway.

'Did you guys wanna stop at Las Vegas on the way back?' said the father as they rolled through California eastward, 'I feel like we didn't get much of a chance to see it on the way here.'

'Alright,' said Klara and Max.

Soon enough as they neared Las Vegas, the landscape turned orange and barren once more.

'Make sure you close all the windows,' warned Mr. Fritz. 'We'll keep the AC on. It's about to get hot.' Low and behold the temperature increased as they drove into the desert, different shrubs and cacti the only life to be found. Eventually 'Red Rock Canyon' came into the distance, a famous landmark for having outstanding natural beauty.

'Can we stop and take pictures of the canyon?' said Mrs. Fritz, about a mile off from the rock formation, the evening approaching. The warm wind passed through as they got out, Mrs. Fritz pulling out her DSLR camera snapping photos of the red and vibrant coloured rock…

Suddenly there was a '*boom*' sound in the distance.

'Aren't these rocks amazing?' said Mrs. Fritz, carrying on snapping photos from her camera.

Max quickened his senses, waiting for a similar sound… Then came the sound of a screeching missile, like a loud firework.

'David!' shouted Max.

'Run!' he shouted, a nearby missile narrowly missing the SUV as it tore into the earth. The explosion flipped the SUV over and back onto its wheels. Luckily the four had scattered

141

into different directions as soon as they heard Max shout, the missile narrowly missing the car.

The familiar sound of David's Jetpack rang through the air as he soared low over the panic-stricken family. 'Get to the car!' shouted Max. The three obeyed immediately.

'Max, get in!' cried Mr. Fritz as he started the engine.

'No, I'll be fine here,' he shouted, 'Drive to Las Vegas. Call the police and tell them David Cohen has returned. Quickly!' he shouted. Max looked up as David Cohen started swooping down towards them from the sky.

Mr. Fritz hit the gas as he drove off into the distance.

Double-taking David Cohen swerved up into the air, seeing his prey had split into two.

Staying with Max he swerved and spiralled into the sky getting ready for another attack on Max who stood helpless from below. Cohen, keeping a distance away from Max, kept him in view at all times. David Cohen swooped down on Max once more, the turrets spinning, as Max ran, jumping into the distance, the bullets from the turrets tearing up the desert floor.

Max watched as David spiralled back into the sky.

David realised quickly that to get at Max without Max hijacking his jetpack, he would have to stay a sufficient distance away from him and yet not give him enough time for him to avoid his missiles.

Cohen reigned havoc upon Max as Max ran and ran, dodging the missiles by only an inch of his teeth, the dirt flying up, the road being destroyed, craters forming in the earth behind him.

Cohen grimaced as he watched Max continually dance and avoid the rockets that were fired down on him from the desert floor. Max looked up as Cohen rose into the air, preparing to swoop down on him again…

Max, knowing he must do something, ran towards Las Vegas, Cohen beginning to swoop down on Max. Max could hear the engines of Cohen's jetpack come ever closer to him, Max running along the desert floor.

Knowing he must do something, Max closed his eyes. Max jumped high into the air, backflipping, awaiting the sound of the jetpack directly behind him. He flew into the air narrowly missing the jetpack swooping downwards at him….. Max landing directly on its back!

Max clambered to stay on the jetpack, his jump and perfect timing paying off. Cohen grimaced as he felt the thud of Max on his back.

In anger, Cohen turned around, away from the direction of Las Vegas city, Max hanging onto Cohen's jetpack, Cohen flying further into the desert.

The night sky started to appear, the red-hot sun being held down by the stars, David zooming through the sky, away from Las Vegas, through the desert. Knowing that Max wouldn't give up holding onto the jetpack, Cohen decided to fly directly upwards again, this time gaining as much speed as possible.

As they climbed into the air Max looked down to his right and saw Las Vegas growing smaller in the distance and what appeared to be four small flying dotted shapes coming over to their direction from the city. Down to his left was what appeared to be a residential area across the vast desert, the lights of the houses sparkling in the distance with what appeared to be an electric power station next to it. Max clung onto dear life as David soared higher and higher into the sky, the desert becoming smaller as they rocketed upwards. Passing the clouds they rocketed further still, the stars becoming clearer and clearer. Max, afraid to look down now, kept his eye focused on the front of the jetpack.

Max, still holding firm to the edge of the jetpack fighter plane, waited for David to turn around, but still he climbed, the G-force heavy and brutal.

Eventually Cohen let go of the engines and let the jetpack freefall as they commenced the most death-defying drop. Down they fell to the ground, the G-force and everything hitting Max all at once. Down they fell through the sky, passing the clouds, the desert floor becoming clearer and clearer with every second. And as they approached the desert, the glow of the city came into view once more, the residential village and the substation also there directly below them. And as they fell... Max had an idea... Attempting the impossible, he jumped from the jetpack as it neared the ground, pushing its trajectory into the direction of the substation. He leapt as far as he could, the jetpack falling, the violent push panicking David as his jetpack began to spin out of control and towards the power station. Max landed on the ground tumbling like tumbleweed as he spun onto the desert floor. There were a few moments of nothingness until behind him he could hear the crackle and the sound of electricity going out of control...

Getting to his feet he turned around and watched as in the distance sparks flew everywhere, the electricity from the substation consuming the jetpack... and David Cohen. Max watched as the electrical charges and electric bolts threw themselves into a storm of anger, the sparks and the electricity creating an explosion like Max had never seen.

Max looked over at the city of Las Vegas as it glowed in the distance. The sound of the helicopters came from far away, the sound of their whirring and chopping nearing, Max squinting his eyes looking back at the black figures kicking up the dust as they started to land.

'Max... is that you?' called one of the men from the helicopters rushing out to him, not too far in the distance.

18

Mrs. Fritz turned on the TV as she watched the news. 'David Cohen, the man behind the terror of the Chicago Parade and the explosion at Battery Park in New York City has officially deceased. With what began as—'
Mrs. Fritz turned to the next channel.

******

There in Lincoln Park the cameras were all focused on Max. It was time for Max's public presentation in Chicago City,

Max now a verified teenage superhero. Children and adults watched from around the appointed areas in the field of the park. There in the middle of the crowds was Max with a good hundred metres or so of space in front of him, people watching attentively as all the journalists, the families, the crowds were silent. Then Max ran, and ran and ran, then finally with all his might he jumped into the air, his body releasing from the ground as he soared higher and higher, the cameras adjusting their angle, cameras flashing and snapping. There Klara, Mr. Fritz and Chuck watched from the crowd, the crowd cheering, Klara cheering, Chuck cheering, Mr. Fritz cheering, Mrs. Fritz cheering from the living room.

ABOUT THE AUTHOR

Thomas John Crossley writes from the suburbs of London, England in Berkshire. Tom loves to read the classics as well as anything commercial that grabs his attention.

Tom has been working as an English Tutor for 3 years. Some of his other jobs have been in retail as well as touring with a professional Irish Dance company as an Irish Dancer.

tjcrossley.wordpress.com

———

Cover designed by Freepik @CallMeDeathFromAbove

freepik.com

Printed in Great Britain
by Amazon

25462062R00088